I0747680

THE
AWAKENING

THE
AWAKENING

a novella

* * *

S C O T T   W .   F E D O R

Published by Coyote Crest, LLC
Westlake, Ohio

Library of Congress Control Number: 2023910192

ISBN: 978-1-7330810-3-0 (paperback)
ISBN: 978-1-7330810-4-7 (ebook)

Printed in the United States of America

Cover design by Ryan Mulford

scottwfedor.com

1 3 5 7 9 10 8 6 4 2

First Edition: July 2023

For Ronin

"Two possibilities exist: either we are alone in the Universe or we are not. Both are equally terrifying."

– Arthur C Clarke

CONTENTS

AUTHOR'S NOTE

During my senior year of high school, I took a creative writing class in which the goal was to write a novel.

The only requirement was that every day we had to write something, nothing special, just write something.

We were told not to worry about punctuation, grammar, or any other type of syntax, just get the words down on paper.

I sat in front of a word processor every night after football practice and just wrote.

Although I had a general idea of what the story was about, I decided to just let the characters and their actions take me where they would. (Not exactly the best way to write a story.)

At the end of the semester, I had the first draft of *The Awakening*. It was rough and needed to be refined, but I had written a novel. Well, technically a (long) short story, or novella.

What you are about to read is the original story. Sure, I cleaned up all the typos and grammar issues (and there were a lot) but I left the story, characters, and plot lines completely intact.

It is what I transcribed three decades ago as a kid in my late teens.

My goal in publishing this novella all these years later, besides selling a million copies, is to preserve the integrity of the original work.

And I have done that.

Admittedly, this is not my best writing. Far from it. The story would benefit from being culled, tightened, and properly paced. It reads like the work of a novice who is new to the craft of writing.

Because that is exactly what it is.

This book's purpose is not meant to appeal to the masses or set the science fiction genre ablaze. Rather, it exists to provide the reader with a glimpse into the mind of an adolescent who thought it would be neat to write a novel.

Over the past thirty years, there have been several stories, films, and other narratives that have a similar theme to my story. However, as you read this novella, keep in mind that those works did not exist when this story was conceived and written. I'd like to think I was somewhat ahead of the curve.

Then again, it's a big curve.

The Awakening is a bizarre story, and I have no recollection of how I even came up with the idea for it. The average reader might find its contents to be off-putting and somewhat shocking. Honestly, it's not exactly something I would choose to write today, as I find it a bit too macabre for my taste.

However, it was my first major writing assignment.

It was fun. I learned a lot. I wanted to share it.

I hope you enjoy it.

CHAPTER 1

The loud and obnoxious shrill of the alarm clock pierced the morning stillness and filled the room with its unpleasant tone.

Dallas Easton slowly awakened to a new day and a chance at a brand-new start.

Outside his window, the city could be heard as it too came to life with the hum of car motors and the buzz of pedestrian traffic stirring the air.

It was 7:30 on a Friday morning.

Dallas reached over and tapped the alarm clock.

In no hurry to rush off to work, Dallas took his time as he got out of bed. As his feet searched the floor for his slippers, a faint crying noise could be heard from the guest bedroom.

He recognized the noise immediately.

His three-month-old Rottweiler, Forrest, had accidentally locked itself in the spare bedroom all night and was now anxious to be free.

In a moment of serendipity, Dallas had discovered the pup at a local hardware store a few weeks earlier. The shop owner's dog had given birth, and a fresh litter of puppies greeted customers with their yaps at the checkout station.

Affixed to the makeshift pen was a homemade sign that read: FREE PUPPIES.

Having always desired a pet of his own, Dallas inquired about the puppies with the shopkeeper, who was more than eager to get the runts off his hands. Ten minutes later, Dallas exited the store with a fresh supply of carpenter nails, wood glue, trim board, and an all too energetic puppy.

It didn't take long for the pair to become best friends, and Dallas was rarely separated from Forrest, except while at work. And, of course, on the rare occasions when the critter locked himself in the adjoining bedroom.

Reading the morning paper wasn't necessarily a necessity for Dallas. Since he noticed he was running late for work, he quickly got dressed. He hadn't planned on staying out late the previous night, and his eyes were feeling the effect of only a few hours of sleep.

He squirted a few drops of Clearview into each eye, gargled some mouthwash, and hastily left for work.

The firm where Dallas worked, Herzig and Statton, was a small boutique law firm with only two partners. He had worked there for less than six months and had been tagged as an up and comer, and one to watch. However, arriving late was certainly not the way he wanted to get noticed.

Although he was not yet an attorney, his job duties dictated otherwise. Dallas was still considered an aide who had all the comforts of an attorney, but just hadn't passed the bar exam yet. He was scheduled to take the test next month.

"Good morning, Mr. Easton," his secretary, Claire, beamed as he stepped out of the elevator onto the twenty-ninth floor.

"Good morning, Claire. Any messages?"

"As a matter of fact, Mr. Easton, Mr. Taylor asked if you could call him when you got in. He's already called several times this morning."

"Thank you, Claire," Dallas said as he hurried down the hall to his office.

What the hell could Brian Taylor want at 9:15 in the morning?

Dallas picked up the phone and punched in Brian's number, which was already programmed into his speed dialing.

"Good morning. Sherwood Enterprises. How may I direct your call?" a soft voice answered as the call was connected.

"Brian Taylor, please," Dallas replied.

"One moment, please."

A few seconds later an even more timid voice spoke into the receiver.

"Hello?"

"Brian," Dallas replied, "I just got in. There was a message to call you."

"Dallas, where were you last night? I tried calling you all night but got no answer."

"I was out. Is something wrong?" Dallas asked.

"You really need to get over here now. It's rather important," he responded.

"What's going on?"

"Just hurry. How fast can you be here?" Brian asked.

"I don't know, ten minutes. Is something wrong?"

But before Dallas could finish his sentence, Brian had already hung up the phone.

Figuring it would be faster to walk, Dallas took the back stairs onto West Haven Boulevard.

Brian worked two blocks away for a company that was in the process of being bought out by Calvin Industries, a multi-million-dollar manufacturer of home furnishings.

Rumor had it that the buyout was going to take place within the week, and Dallas wondered if that was the reason for Brian's excitement.

Dallas and Brian had been friends since their

second year together at Princeton. After graduation they had both gone on to bigger and better things, but at present, their futures appeared to be heading in opposite directions.

Dallas emerged from his building and stepped onto West Haven. A few minutes later he stood in the lobby of Brian's place of work as he waited for the elevator.

Dallas surveyed the expansive area. It was the first time he had been in the Sherwood Building since they had remodeled it.

The white linoleum floor was covered with a massive Persian rug that was adorned with green and yellow floral designs. The carpet stretched from the front desk to the revolving doors and spanned from wall to wall.

It clashed badly with pale-blue walls that were festooned with giant tapestries from a bygone era.

Large, chunky, crystal chandeliers dangled from the ceiling and refracted what little sunlight shone through the building's glass façade.

Dallas made his way to the bank of elevators and waited. The doors soon opened, and he stepped inside. He was alone, and the overwhelming space of the elevator seemed to engulf him.

Less than a minute later, a ding alerted Dallas that he had arrived at Brian's floor.

Upon his exit, Dallas was immediately struck by the eerie silence that replaced the usual din he was accustomed to. Normally this place was somewhat of a madhouse, at least every time Dallas had previously visited Brian.

However, on this particular morning, the faint sound of rustling papers was all that could be heard as Dallas made his way to the receptionist's desk. The skeleton crew of employees halfheartedly glanced up to see who had just stepped onto their floor.

Dallas inched his way over to the receptionist.

"I'm here to see Brian Taylor," he whispered so as not to upset the strange ambience that permeated the floor.

"Excuse me?" the receptionist said, looking up.

"Brian Taylor," he repeated, "I talked to him a few minutes ago, and he asked me to come over to see him."

"Are you Dallas?" she asked.

"Yes."

"He's expecting you, Mr. Easton. His office is right down the hall, second door on the left." She pointed a pencil in the direction.

"Thank you."

Something has to be wrong.

Dallas made his way down the hall to Brian's office and knocked on the door.

"Yeah. Come on in," a voice responded.

Dallas turned the doorknob, but it was locked.

"Uh, Brian, door's locked."

Seconds later the door slowly swung open.

"Brian, is everything all right? I got here as fast as I could. You sounded kinda weird on the phone. I didn't know what to make of it."

Brian proceeded back to his paperwork-cluttered desk and gingerly situated himself in his leather swivel chair.

"Dallas," he said as he glanced around the room at the stacks of boxes lining the walls, "we've been bought out."

"I know," Dallas began, "you told me yesterday. Brian. Are you okay? You don't seem yourself."

Brian slowly got up from his chair and moved towards the window, taking baby steps, as if he was still an infant. He positioned himself on the windowsill and stared out onto the busy streets below.

Brian sat on the ledge, his hands trembling as his fingers fumbled with the window locks. Eventually, he successfully unlocked the window.

Immediately, a cool breeze filtered into the room and tossed Brian's short, brown hair around.

He began to unbutton his shirt, paying careful attention to each button as if it was the most important task he would ever complete.

"Dallas," he said, "there's something I need to tell you."

"What is it?"

"Dallas," he replied again, this time a bit softer.

"Brian, what the hell is the matter?"

"I'm sorry, Dallas," Brian said as he took his shirt off and gazed out the window.

Dallas walked over to Brian, who now had tears in his eyes.

"Brian. If something's wrong, tell me. Please, I can help you."

Brian wiped the tears from his eyes with the back of his hand.

"Dallas, remember how I told you about the buyout and how Calvin was planning on utilizing our facilities to manufacture furniture?"

"We just talked about it the other day," Dallas responded, somewhat confused.

Brian continued, "Well, I couldn't let that happen. I knew there was no way this deal could hold. It just sounded too good to be true. And I was right. After some digging around, I found out Calvin Industries was planning on breaking us up. At least that's what I heard through the grapevine.

"They were planning on scamming my boss, Mr. Lionel. He's such an innocent guy who was taken advantage of. They forced him into signing those papers. They told him he would lose everything if he didn't. I owe this company a lot. If it wasn't for this job, I'd have nothing."

"Brian, I'm sure he wasn't forced into signing anything. This could be a good thing for Sherwood."

Brian continued to ramble, "So in order to save the company, I sent a memo to Eckhart, the CEO of Calvin, and told him Mr. Lionel was reneging on the deal."

"You did what!" an astonished Dallas asked.

"As you can imagine, that didn't go over too well."

"Please tell me you're joking," Dallas implored.

"And after he received it, he called Lionel and told him that I was planning on screwing the company over. Even though it was Eckhart who was going to liquidate the entire firm by selling it off in small fractions."

"Brian, take a deep breath and relax," Dallas said as he extended his hand onto Brian's shoulder.

Brian just continued, "He was going to eliminate Sherwood, and all its employees. Hundreds of men and women, fired. Left without a job, no money to support their families. What was I to do? So I told Eckhart to go to hell and that there was no way I would let him go through with it.

"Well, today I got a notice demanding I resign by the end of the week. Dallas, what am I going to do? Sherwood is on their side. I'm terminated. And not only that, no one in their right mind would even think about hiring me after the stunt I pulled. I'm finished. There's nothing left for me."

Dallas tried to offer some reassurance, "Brian, it's going to be all right. I'll help you."

Brian started to sob more heavily.

Dallas did his best to console his friend. He

offered to place a call to Calvin Industries the following morning to see if he could smooth things over.

The gesture seemed to temporarily offer Brian some reassurance.

Back at his office, Dallas continued to think about Brian's situation. Although he had offered to help, there was no way he could. If he were to insert himself into the situation, it would only make matters worse. Not just for Brian, but also for Dallas and his firm.

Herzig and Statton was acting as lead counsel on Calvin's acquisition of Sherwood.

Dallas could not let Brian find that out.

Before he left work for the evening, Dallas placed a call to Brian to see how he was doing. He did his best to reassure him that he would see what he could do.

Brian, relieved, conveyed to Dallas how grateful he was for his help. He even went so far as to tell Dallas he finally started to feel a little bit of hope.

However, Dallas knew Brian had no hope.

When he arrived home, Dallas took a long shower. Afterwards, feeling revived, he called Brian's office, but received a recording telling him no such number existed.

Impossible.

He called five more times, and each time got the same response.

Finally, in desperation, he called the operator.

"I'm sorry, sir, but there is no number listed that

matches the one you gave me," the operator said.

The phone fell from Dallas's hand onto the floor.

Dallas was confused.

Why was Brian fired so promptly?

The referendum he'd been given stated he was to finish out the week.

Do they know I tried to help him?

He repeatedly tried to call Brian at his home but got no answer.

Dallas needed to clear his head. He took Forrest for a long walk while he mulled things over in his mind.

In the morning, he would call Brian.

There had to be some kind of explanation.

After he locked everything up for the night, Dallas went to his room and collapsed into his bed. Thoughts of Brian bounced around in his head as he tried to fall asleep. In the morning he would go see him again. He would figure something out.

Dallas closed his eyes and fell asleep.

CHAPTER 2

In another galaxy some 200 billion light years away, on a planet very similar to Earth, Sallad awoke after a tremendous night's sleep. He slept comfortably, knowing that today was finally the day when he would test his new experiment.

Sallad lived on Epacseon, a parallel planet to Earth. Epacseon was not a chartered planet, and had never been seen by anyone, other than Epacseonites.

The closest neighboring planet to Epacseon was Xenorusa, which was thirteen million light years away from Pluto, and increased its distance by threefold every Earth year.

Similar to Earth, Epacseon had one moon, and revolved around a Tullib, a massive red ball of rock that contained all the energy for its solar system.

Its inhabitants also spoke unique languages native to different parts of the planet. However, the region where Sallad lived was strictly English-speaking.

He had lived on Epacseon for twenty-eight years. He worked as a techno-scientist, one who studied the atmosphere of neighboring stars and planets.

Sallad made his way to the bathroom, prepared the shower, and readied himself for work. A full day of undertaking awaited him, and he needed to get to his office as early as possible.

Two weeks earlier Sallad accidentally came across a very bizarre, yet fascinating discovery while at Aspirion, his place of employment. While working in the records department one day, he serendipitously misplaced an important document in the electronic archive that housed all the company research.

Sallad had just completed a study on one of Epacseon's neighboring binary star systems and logged his findings into the computer. However, he mistakenly catalogued the data in the Gasderwy directory, which was only supposed to be accessed when data studies were incomplete.

Realizing his mistake, he quickly tried to retrieve the file. Unfortunately, the file data log had been shuffled around due to the above average computer use that day, and as a result, Sallad was forced to conduct a query to discover the log.

As he carefully scanned the Gasderwy directory,

he stumbled across an unfinished data log entitled "Sublime-Hypotracing."

Immediately, the data log piqued Sallad's curiosity and led him to investigate further, even though he knew it was a violation to access any file he did not create. In his mind, the infringement was warranted.

What he found was incredibly fascinating, and something that would set in motion a course of events that would forever alter his life, as well as the lives of others.

The file's contents detailed a comprehensive and furtive study of subconscious illusioning, an experimental technique projected onto individuals who dealt with insomnia.

The analysis demonstrably indicated that through micro-frying, it was possible to link the subliminal reality of an individual who was having trouble sleeping, to a dream state that allowed that person the ability to access a subconscious mindset.

The file had been stored in the Gasderwy directory since the experiment had only been tested once, and on another star for that matter.

In other words, much more extensive research was needed. The trial had also proven to be extremely dangerous, and as a result was marked for obsolescence and scheduled to be destroyed.

Enthralled with the data, Sallad went ahead and transferred the file to his personal Interface computer. He then made sure to delete the original file so that no one would ever be able to trace its existence.

More importantly, he erased his digital footprints and left no indication that he had ever accessed the file.

Since discovering the study, Sallad had spent the entirety of his time researching its contents and posited theories. He diligently dissected every morsel of data contained within it.

The study's findings unequivocally proved it was entirely possible to control someone's dreams if the right set of conditions existed. However, the dream tampering, known as micro-frying, could only be used to produce somnia, and should never under any circumstances be induced upon an unwitting subject who had not provided consent.

Sallad had stayed late into the night every day after work and repeatedly pored over the file.

Furthermore, through his detailed analysis of the evidence, he discovered that given the right conditions in the ideal atmosphere, one could do more than just induce the sweet dreams that would put someone to sleep.

The research inferred that one could not only control when the test object would sleep, but also what dreams would be introduced.

By countering the micro-frying sequence with an equilibrium sequence, and altering the cerebral balance of the patient, the controller could temporarily transport its subject into a subliminal dimension that had the ability to be manipulated.

Once in that dimension, by regulating the equilibrium state, it was up to the controller how long the dreams would be induced.

Sallad kept a journal in which he transcribed his findings. For two weeks he exhausted himself analyzing and reanalyzing the data to substantiate the study's theory:

Given the right specimen, inhabiting the right conditions, an artificially constructed subconscious reality could be imposed upon said subject.

The morning had finally arrived.

After what had seemed like months of tedious work and extensive research, today was the day Sallad planned to progress to the next phase of the project.

On the shuttle to work, Sallad mentally rehearsed the final details, ad nauseam. He needed to make sure no stone was left unturned.

First, he would run the mind-frying sequence through the Interface computer once more to familiarize the machine with the data log he would be using.

Next, he would connect an intra-circuit wire with a transfer node that would allow him to tap into the energy field of other planets.

That connection would enable him to draw from the planet's favorable conditions and run them through a central Kijyerty electrode, which would connect his computer with the planet's atmosphere, and thus link him to the entire planet.

Sallad stepped off the shuttle and onto the pristine

white pavement that surrounded his office building. The pavement was punctuated with sections of lush grass and bright, green trees. Everything on Epacseon, including the environment, was state-of-the-art.

His office was situated in a thirteen-hundred-story glass structure that towered above the clouds. He took the Tram to the building's entrance and then proceeded to hover-transport to his floor.

Sallad was ecstatic.

Today, he would embark on a revolutionary form of science that had never been executed or even thought to be attempted by anyone, not even the elite pioneers in the field of Harnessing.

He was going to program a series of dreams into an individual's mind that only he could control.

Upon passing the cantina situated on his floor, Sallad grabbed a cup of Gotcha, a highly concentrated and enriched form of caffeine.

He tossed the substance down the back of his throat. Surprisingly, it tasted pretty good. He was not a fan of Gotcha's astringent taste, but today he even opted for a second cup.

The second cup of Gotcha was even more refreshing than the first, and Sallad felt euphoriated.

Quickly, as if up against an unrelenting deadline, he entered through his office passport window and tossed his briefcase on a nearby chair. He proceeded to his electronatable and flipped a switch that powered up the vast number of machines in his office.

Immediately, a humming sound whirred inside the walls, signaling that the electrical hatch had opened. Moments later the room was illuminated with machine banks of blinking lights and receptive sensors.

Sallad smiled. He took pride in his technological wizardry.

On Epacseon, the field of Harnessing was highly respected. A career as a Harnesser was not only lucrative, but also one of the more esteemed positions that one could hope to aspire to. And when it came to Harnessing, Sallad was one of the best.

He had graduated with tri-honors from Gabriel, the finest institute on the planet. Its founder, Plax Gabriel, had envisioned and designed the prestigious university to train Epacseonites to harness energy.

Admittance to Gabriel was a highly competitive endeavor. Its bylaws mandated that any individual who sought acceptance be recommended by a Master, an expertly trained and educated leader in the field of Energynomics.

Recommendations were not easy to attain.

Sallad had studied at Gabriel for eight years, the maximum, and graduated with the highest rank in his class, which earned him tri-honors. He could have worked anywhere his heart desired and chose to work at Aspirion.

He sat down behind his desk and flipped on the Interface's monitor. After he completed the identification protocols, he entered his password and began to set up the data log for his experiment.

Sallad got up and walked over to his briefcase, unsnapped it, and retrieved a disk from it.

The disk.

He popped it into the Interface.

He sat and waited.

The machine only took a few seconds to process the information, but it felt like an eternity to Sallad. Finally, the screen lit up with information on micro-frying. He quickly entered the data log number for coding.

"Good morning," the computer greeted him, "please press the homing bar to establish authenticity."

Sallad pressed the bar that recorded his prints.

"To access file, please press the homing bar and begin."

Sallad pressed the bar once more and started inputting information into the computer. He also made sure to set up an anti-tracking device to ensure no one would be able to trace his modem.

Although the probability was quite low that his sequence could ever be traced, Sallad was unwilling to take that chance.

Once the anti-tracking had been established, he entered the code for his new file, which he had changed from "Sublime-Hypotracing" to "Food Vegetation" so that the file could not be identified in the rare event that someone accessed his computer.

Sallad stared at the monitor.

He accessed the file's contents and scoured the log for the proper place to enter the next set of coordinates for further mapping. He entered the coordinates.

The subconscious illusioning sequence populated the screen. He reviewed the theory a final time and then permanently entered it into the Interface's memory.

Now that the program's foundation had been properly installed, Sallad could finally proceed with what he had worked so diligently on over the previous weeks.

Sallad loaded the equilibrium sequence he had artfully devised into the computer's memory bank. He displayed both sequences side-by-side on the monitor in front of him.

The most critical step in the process now awaited.

Sallad carefully took his time and overlaid the equilibrium sequence's mapping onto the subconscious illusioning sequence.

That action created a digital patchwork of nano bytes that morphed into a new sequence he called The Awakening.

Sallad now had a sequence capable of launching an individual into an unbalanced state and subjecting that person to a false or distorted subliminal reality. More importantly, he had the means to control the sequence.

Finally, Sallad was ready to begin the mind-frying experiment.

Sallad reached into his desk, where he kept his

Harnesser's manual. He turned to page eighty-one, where it described the transfer wire. Sallad carefully read through the manual and followed the directions exactly as they were stated.

He turned on his SystemsLink computer, an auxiliary machine that worked alongside his Interface. While he waited for the machine to come online and sync with the Interface, he paid a visit to the storeroom at the end of the hall and extracted from its supply shelf a transfer wire. By the time he got back to his office, he was ready to continue.

The directions in the Harnesser's manual called for Sallad to insert one end of the transfer wire into the SystemsLink computer, and the other end into the Interface computer's modem.

Done.

He now had a medium by which to transmit the Kijyerty electrode. It was a rather simple task to establish the transfer wire, and Sallad put the manual back.

He was now ready to initiate the sequence.

Sallad stared at the computers in front of him.

The moment had finally arrived.

He was about to embark upon the most amazing and groundbreaking way to harness electrical currents–he was going to fry them into someone's mind.

Sallad clearly knew that his experimentation with this concept would violate every code of Harnessing, and if he were to get caught, he would be terminated. Perhaps most devastating though, he would lose his Harnessing license and be disgraced among his colleagues.

But the risk was worth it.

If Sallad was able to successfully create a program that enabled a controller to link its subject to his own thoughts, all would be forgiven. At least that is how he justified it to himself.

Sallad was about to make history.

He pressed the Startup key on the Interface.

"Please enter your code number," the computer chimed.

Sallad entered his number, which was the same as his code word, just the numerical version of it. The screen cleared, and Sallad was looking at a blank monitor in front of him.

"Please proceed," commanded the computer.

He pressed the F4 key.

"Sequence activated."

Sallad had just activated the Awakening sequence.

He was about to tap into someone's mind and control their subliminal reality.

Suddenly it occurred to Sallad that throughout all the preparation he had done over the previous weeks, there was one crucial item he had never considered.

Who am I going to test the Awakening on?

Where would he find someone to fry? What kind of subject would he need that would enable him to maximize the full potential of the sequence?

He needed a specimen who was unsuspecting.

But who?

Sallad grew anxious. If he could not activate the sequence soon, he might never again have the opportunity to do so.

Sallad's nerves began to get the best of him, and he had to use the restroom. He proceeded down the hall, oblivious to his surroundings and engrossed in his own world. His mind raced in overdrive as it tried to settle the sole question that tumbled about.

Who am I going to test the Awakening on?

Sallad stepped into the bathroom.

The employee lavatories at Aspirion were quite lavish and each stall was equipped with a telemonitor, a TV-like screen designed to occupy the boredom while doing one's business.

He entered the end stall, closed the door, and sat down. As Sallad watched the screen, the intergalactic weather forecast came on. The forecaster was giving the conditions for the Milky Way galaxy. Suddenly, Sallad was besieged with a brainwave.

I will find my subject in a different galaxy!

Of course! This way if something went wrong, no one could ever trace it back to him. Additionally, the subject would be completely clueless and ignorant of the situation. There would be absolutely no way for him or her to comprehend what was happening.

Sallad even knew the perfect planet. Earth.

He was overcome with such excitement that he hurried out of the bathroom without even flushing the toilet or turning off the telemonitor.

As soon as he got back to his office, he quickly punched up the mind-frying file and typed in the word, "Earth."

Immediately the screen lit up with an abundance of information about the planet. Sallad entered the word "population."

Epacseon was so far ahead of any other civilization when it came to technology, that the mainframes housed the complete listing of every sentient being that existed on every planet across thirteen different galaxies.

Sallad watched in delight as he held down the Arrow key and rifled through all the names of the inhabitants, at a rate of 150,000 names per second. Sallad closed his eyes, held his breath, and pressed Enter.

He had just randomly selected a specimen for his experiment. An unsuspecting subject who would never know that its mind was about to be hijacked and all control of its life ceded to Sallad.

He looked at the screen to see the name of the hapless soul who had just been identified.

Dallas Easton.

"Congratulations, Mr. Easton."

Sallad eagerly entered Easton's identity into the program file. All Sallad had to do now was run the sequence. Thanks to the Kijyerty electrode, the file would be able to electro-locate Dallas and imprint the Awakening sequence on him.

Sallad took a deep breath.

Once he pressed the key, in roughly eighteen hours, the time it would take the Kijyerty's electricity to reach Earth, the sequence would be initiated.

Sallad inputted his name as the head navigator into the program file.

He slowly exhaled and pressed the homing bar.

The sequence was activated.

CHAPTER 3

Dallas was astir after a surprisingly great night of sleep. He felt refreshed and rejuvenated. Before hopping in the shower, he took Forrest for a nice long walk. When he arrived back home, he sat down and read the paper, a rarity for him.

It was Saturday. Dallas planned to use the day to catch up on some much needed and long overdue work around the house. Feeling energized after the walk, he decided to forgo the shower and went upstairs to don his work clothes.

Once in the garage, Dallas brought out the ladder and leaned it against the side of the house. The first order of business was to attack the leaf-clogged gutters. This was the first time he had attempted to clean them in six months, and they were in dire need of a good cleaning.

Just as Dallas started to clear the muck away, the phone rang. He climbed down two rungs and jumped the remaining seven feet. He landed hard, twisting his ankle, but he was all right. He scampered inside to answer the phone.

"Hello?"

"Dallas," the familiar voice on the other end was Brian's, "what are you up to?"

"Just cleaning the gutters. How are you doing? Feeling any better?"

"I don't know, I guess I'm okay. I hardly got a wink of sleep, but I'm feeling better."

"That's good to hear," Dallas replied. "Hey, if it will help take your mind off things, you can come over here and help me with the gutters."

"I don't know, man, last time I helped you try to fix your pipes we flooded the entire basement."

"Yeah, I know," Dallas laughed, "but this will be good for you."

"All right. I'll be over in a few minutes."

The phone clicked.

Dallas grabbed a quick glass of water and went back outside and waited for Brian.

The sun shone down intensely upon his bare chest and Dallas grabbed the sunblock that was next to him. As he spread the thick lotion across his chest, a car pulled into the driveway. A tall mustachioed man, dressed in a dark suit, emerged from the car and approached him.

"Are you Dallas Easton?" the man asked.

"Yeah, what can I do you for?" Dallas responded.

"I have a package for you," he replied as he retrieved a clipboard from his car. Then he grabbed a small, brown box adorned with a red bow and walked towards Dallas.

"Here," he extended the clipboard, "sign where it tells you to. I'll put this on the porch."

Dallas was puzzled.

Who would send him a package, and what was it?

He picked up the parcel and carried it inside. Just as he started to open it, Brian's vehicle pulled up. Dallas pushed the box aside and went back outside to greet Brian.

Brian had an odd, yet whimsical look on his face when he stepped out of the car. He was dressed in a blue suit and wearing his Princeton tie.

"Brian," Dallas began, "I said we would be working, but on the roof."

Brian's gaze was firmly affixed upon Dallas. His quirky countenance now portrayed a look that could cut through steel.

"Dallas. Oh, Dallas. Not today or ever again."

"Brian what's the matter with you? Here, sit down." Dallas pointed to a chair, but Brian didn't even budge. "Hey, listen, I'm your best friend. If something's wrong, tell me," Dallas continued.

"Not today," Brian smiled.

Without warning, Brian reached into his coat pocket and pulled out a .38 special handgun. Dallas was astonished.

"Brian, where the hell did you get that? Put that thing away, man. Are you crazy? You could kill somebody with that thing."

"Not today," Brian said.

He pointed the gun at Dallas and fired.

The shot reverberated as a bullet tore through the still morning air.

Dallas fell to the ground and covered his face.

"Not today," Brian repeated once more.

He then got back in his car and drove away.

* * *

Dallas was consumed in complete darkness.

The faint sound of nearby voices could be heard, but try as he might, he could not make out the muffled sounds they spoke.

His body felt hauntingly cold. He tried to scream but was unable to muster the slightest of sounds that was even remotely perceptible.

He tried again. And again. Nothing.

Dallas sensed the weight of a cloth draped atop his body. It felt heavy and suffocating.

"Well, did you get on the horn?" the chief of police asked.

"Yes, Chief," a cop replied, as he slammed the door of his cruiser, which was parked in Dallas's driveway. "The deputy said a gun was found matching the coroner's description of the bullet 'bout a mile down the road."

"Well, where the hell is it?" boomed the chief.

"Forensics picked it up. Running prints."

"Good." The chief looked down at Dallas, "Get this stiff out of here."

Dallas's body was picked up and loaded into the coroner's vehicle. Thoughts hurtled through his mind like bolts of lightning. Slowly, his cognizance restored to its natural state.

But it was too late.

The door slammed shut and the car pulled away.

Dallas was confused.

He remembered talking to Brian.

And then...

And then I was shot. I was shot!

Dallas recalled the events that had transpired. He had been shot by Brian, his best friend. Brian had gone mad. The stress he was under must have finally gotten to him.

He had flipped.

The car turned the corner onto a small dirt road that led back to a tiny hidden building tucked away among the trees. The tires churned up dust as the vehicle slowly made its way along the path.

The car stopped.

Dallas heard footsteps approach the back of the vehicle. The door opened. Small speckles of light poked through the blanket that covered him.

Once again, he tried to scream.

Nothing.

What's wrong?

Who are these people?

Where are they taking me?

Dallas Easton was still alive.

CHAPTER 4

S allad queued in line as he waited for the next Tram to transport him back to his launch that awaited him in the landing depot.

A wry grin accentuated his handsome face.

Mere hours earlier, he had embarked upon arguably the most sensational and cutting-edge experiment of the times, when he had activated his unsanctioned mind-frying sequence.

The Tram arrived and Sallad boarded. He found an empty window seat and plopped down for the short ride to the depot. He watched as Aspirion's office building receded into the distance at a blinding speed.

Sallad could barely contain his excitement.

On the 917th floor of that shiny office building, Sallad had just imprinted his Awakening sequence onto a naïve Earthling and would soon have complete control of his reality.

Provided that Dallas Easton was still alive.

The Tram came to a stop. Sallad quickly exited and made his way to his launch. He was eager to get home for the final few hours of the sequence's activation. His briefcase contained notes he needed to review before he could successfully assume control of Dallas's life.

As soon as Sallad stepped into his house he went to his voicemail machine and pressed the Playback button. Fortunately, there weren't any messages to further delay him from getting to work. He was so anxious to begin that he didn't even change into more comfortable clothes, rather opting to remain in uniform.

Sallad cleared a table in his living room and moved it closer to him. He took a seat in his comforchair and tried his best to relax. Adrenaline coursed through his veins.

To begin, he arranged his paperwork into three different stacks. In the first stack he placed all the papers that contained instructions for what he had already done. The middle stack, perhaps the most critical, contained all the papers that described the next few steps of the sequence, including what must, at all costs, be avoided. Finally, the last stack was the papers that detailed what constituted a successful experiment.

Sallad sat back and took a deep breath. He knew it was going to be a long night, so he got up and went to the kitchen to make some Gotcha. While he waited for the Gotcha, Sallad went back into the living room and picked up the middle stack of papers, which highlighted the critical next steps. He carefully began to read them.

* * *

Dallas repeatedly blinked his eyes.

His body still felt unusually cold. He clenched his fists in desperation as he tried to wriggle free from beneath the blanket atop him.

"Somebody, please, help me. I'm not dead!"

It was no use. No one could hear him.

Dallas Easton was locked away in a metal box, stuffed inside a massive, refrigerated compartment somewhere on the bottom floor of a building. He might as well have been at the bottom of the Mariana Trench.

But then something happened.

He sneezed.

And he heard it.

Overcome with an incredible feeling of hope, he blurted out his name at the top of his lungs, "Dallas."

He cried tears of joy.

He heard his name.

Dallas furiously kicked the metal door that was positioned near his feet.

The coroner and the police chief were in the middle of a conversation in the autopsy room when they heard the banging.

Their heads whipped around in unison to locate the commotion. They were both overcome with utter bewilderment and fright when they realized the noise was on the other side of the locked storage door.

Apparently, a dead guy was trying to escape.

The coroner unlatched the door and opened it.

Right away, a confused and relieved Dallas Easton screamed as he gasped for air.

"What the hell is the matter with you guys?"

The chief and coroner looked on, both completely stunned at what they saw. It took several moments for them to comprehend the situation at hand.

"Jesus, you're alive!" the coroner shouted.

"Of course I'm alive," Easton replied.

"We thought you were dead. I mean, I..." the chief could hardly form a sentence.

"Obviously, I'm not," Dallas confirmed.

Two hours later, Dallas was released from the hospital after an extensive battery of tests had been conducted.

The doctors determined that Dallas's central nervous system had been shocked by the bullet's entry into his body and essentially rebooted itself and propelled him into a five-hour coma.

The chief gave Dallas a ride to the police station.

Once there, it was explained to him that Brian was nowhere to be found; however, a weapon registered to him had been recovered. Dallas did his best to provide the police with a description of Brian, from which they made a composite to circulate throughout the town.

It was late in the evening when Dallas finally arrived home. The magnitude of the day's events weighed heavy on him, and it was difficult for him to comprehend everything that had transpired.

"Sir, it's time for your dinner," the nurse said.

Dallas was still at the hospital.

"What the...Where...Who are you?" Dallas was confused.

"You're at a hospital. Somebody shot you and you were severely wounded. The police found you in your driveway. You've been sleeping for the past two days. It's good to see you awake."

Dallas was in a state of shock.

Something odd was happening inside of him. For some reason he was oblivious to his surroundings.

The nurse leaned across to straighten his pillow.

"Honey, you haven't eaten anything in two days, why don't you try to put something in your stomach."

"I don't know what's going on anymore," Dallas said. "I mean, the last thing I remember was standing in my driveway talking to Brian and he shot me."

"Well, whoever it was," the nurse interrupted, "the police have been asking a lot of questions. Once you've eaten something and gotten some of your strength back, I'm sure they will be in to talk to you. Now, why don't you eat something."

Dallas watched the nurse make up the empty bed beside him and then leave. He stared at the tray of food in front of him. The meal consisted of a tuna sandwich with lettuce, a pickle spear, and a glass of milk.

Dallas was too confused to eat.

He fumbled with the IV attached to his arm.

Outside the door, Dallas could hear voices.

Two men in cheap suits and expensive sunglasses barged into the room.

"Dallas Easton," the taller man said, "my name is Detective Braddock and this is my partner, Detective Hinckley. We're here to ask you a few questions. How are you feeling?"

The detective didn't wait for a response. "Good. Well then, let's get down to business. Two days ago, you were shot at close range with a .38 special at approximately 10:30 a.m. We were able to recover the weapon, but forensics found no match on the prints. Mr. Easton, do you have any idea who shot you or might want to cause you harm?"

Dallas thought for a minute.

Why did Brian shoot me with no warning?

Was he in some trouble he couldn't talk about?

Or is he actually crazy?

"No," Dallas responded.

"Are you sure, Mr. Easton?"

"Yes, I think so."

"Mr. Easton, the nurse told us you mentioned the name Brian. Is there any connection between Brian and the suspect?"

Dallas was very quiet.

"Mr. Easton," the other detective said, "we need all the clues we can get. Now, if this Brian is the man who shot you, we need to know so we can stop him from doing any further damage to himself or anyone else. Mr. Easton, did Brian shoot you?"

Dallas looked at the stoic faces of the detectives.

"Yes," he softly whispered.

"Thank you for the cooperation," Braddock said. "Now, Mr. Easton, can you tell us Brian's last name?"

"Taylor. Brian Taylor."

As soon as Dallas had said the words, he felt like he had made a huge mistake.

The detectives thanked him and left.

The next day, Dallas was discharged from the hospital. The doctors explained that the bullet had lodged itself into his neck and the risk of removing it outweighed the risk of leaving it.

They told him he should consider himself lucky.

Yeah, real lucky, he thought to himself.

It was Wednesday evening when Dallas finally arrived home.

To his dismay, Forrest was missing.

Dallas was completely devastated and spent hours as he drove around the city hoping to locate him.

Unfortunately, his search was futile, and Dallas was absolutely devastated. He loved that dog.

Forrest was gone.

Dallas sat exhausted at the kitchen table, barely able to keep his eyes open. The toll of the previous several days weighed heavy on him.

He laid his head down on his folded arms and tried to collect his thoughts and rebalance himself. But it was no use. There were too many questions that needed answers before he could ever find any balance.

Next to him, atop the table, lay the package he had received shortly before he was shot. He eyed it for several minutes before he decided to open it.

Dallas peered inside.

It was a small book titled *The Awakening*, by Peter von Hoffman.

He cautiously flipped the front cover open and noticed a handwritten inscription scrawled in blue ink.

"To Dallas. May your time on Earth be well spent until you journey onward into another life of surprises."

It was signed by Brian.

Dallas only grew more confused.

The bizarre events of late could not be ignored, but he was simply too tired to try to rationalize anything, let alone the mind of Brian. He would try to make sense of everything in the morning.

For now, he just needed sleep.

CHAPTER 5

Sallad was stretched out in his comforchair perusing the paperwork that detailed the idiosyncrasies of the Awakening sequence.

It had been almost twelve hours since he had imprinted the sequence upon Dallas; however, more time was needed before he could fully assume the reins of Easton's reality.

Sallad sifted through piece after piece of material as he searched for the information he needed. According to his research, he would only be able to operate the sequence from a terminal, which was required to properly relay any cerebral resonance to the subject, in this case Dallas Easton.

Luckily, he had a makeshift terminal at his home that he would be able to use and not have to rely on always running the sequence from his office.

Once he was attached to the terminal and his maiden instructions were programmed, all subsequent instructions would reach Dallas within minutes as opposed to hours.

Even though the instructions were made up of millions of electrical nano bytes, they would not take the usual eighteen hours to reach Dallas, due to a chipper device, or homing device, that would be attached to each instruction.

Sallad eyed the clock.

It was early morning and he had worked straight through the night. However, he felt more alive than if he had gotten a full night of rest due to the extraordinary amount of Gotcha he had drunk.

He gathered up his papers, stuffed them in his briefcase, and headed out for another day of work.

Behind his desk, the door locked, Sallad was ready to send his first instruction.

He sat in stillness.

It occurred to him that he had spent weeks designing the sequence, but never once bothered to think about what he would do with it.

He continued to rack his brain for the perfect instruction that would commence the sequence.

He needed something to break the ice.

But what?

As he thought about what he wanted to

accomplish with the Awakening, he had the horrible reckoning that he didn't even know what his purpose for creating the sequence was.

Panic gripped him.

He told himself to calm down.

It had been a long night, and he was a little fried, his mind had been in overdrive for quite some time.

Sallad took a few deep breaths.

He reminded himself that he was on the verge of proving his discovery, a discovery that would be hailed as the most significant breakthrough in Harnessing.

The stress he placed on himself trying to create the perfect instruction was causing too much anxiety, and Sallad resigned himself to just start off with something simple. Besides, something small and innocent would also not arouse suspicion in his Earthly victim.

Sallad called up the sequence on his monitor.

He keyed in a benign instruction.

The first mind-fry Sallad would transmit to Dallas Easton's mind was a vision of the Tullib, something that only Epacseonites had ever seen.

Sallad inputted the instruction and sent it.

He couldn't help but laugh at how easy it was to execute the program he had designed.

It only took a few keystrokes.

The hard part, he knew, would be exluminating the instructions once sent. In other words, every instruction that was imprinted would permanently reside in the control's mind unless he deleted it.

Sallad paced his office.

He peered out the window, which was an entire wall made of glass that afforded him a vast vantage of the surroundings.

Epacseon was a beautiful planet, especially the sector where Sallad lived. Although the floor he worked on was extremely high up in the building, trees still lingered in front of him. All forms of flora were more than twenty times greater on Epacseon than on any other planet. The Epacseonites had learned to care for nature in such a way that it would never die, rather just continue to perpetually grow.

The deep azure sky stretched forever and kept sentry over the lush grasslands and rolling hills of bright, green sod.

Sallad felt the warmth of the Tullib throughout his body. Its energy easily penetrated the thick glass wall and encapsulated his body, further stoking the euphoric sensation that now coursed through him.

Epacseon. What a great planet!

Sallad checked his Interface computer. The instruction had already reached Dallas. All that was left to do was to press the homing bar.

He pressed it.

Billions and billions of light years away, an intense red beam of light suddenly flashed across Dallas's eyes as he brushed his teeth. The powerful image caused him to immediately drop his toothbrush into the sink.

He rubbed his eyes and, half-blinded, picked up his brush and washed it off. Dallas figured his body was telling him he needed more sleep.

The flash came again, only this time even more vivid and intense. Dallas stumbled backwards and had to grab the corner of the sink to steady himself.

"Damn. These pain meds are really messing with me," he mumbled aloud as he staggered to his bedroom.

He collapsed onto his bed and closed his eyes. Again, without warning, a blinding red spot jolted him, causing him to utter a faint cry of torment.

Dallas tried to close his eyes, but each time he did, a bright flash of red light blinded him. Dallas felt as if he was trying to sleep with his eyes open while someone shined an industrial-strength flashlight from only a few inches away.

Dallas started to retreat to the bathroom to grab some Clearview but crumpled to the floor before he could make it there.

He couldn't even see two feet in front of him.

The onslaughts of burning red light were so bright that it hurt to have vision.

He felt his way against the walls and made it to the bathroom. He finished off the Clearview, dispersing the rest of its contents into each eye. Dallas blinked his teary eyes and wiped away the Clearview that dripped down his face.

Sallad paced back and forth behind the Interface.

He had no way to see Dallas and could only wonder if his instruction had taken effect and worked.

Sallad had spent so much time researching the sequence, though, that he convinced himself it had in fact worked. He sat down behind the desk and pressed the homing bar a second time to stop the instruction.

"Are you sure?" the monitor read.

Sallad confirmed his intention.

The Tullib instruction was terminated, but only temporarily, as it would remain in Dallas's mind as an illumination. Unless Sallad permanently deleted the instruction, a process known as exlumination, he had the ability to reactivate it anytime at his discretion.

Sallad turned off the computer and forced himself to finish some work that needed to be completed for his supervisor by the end of the day.

Dallas sat on the edge of his bed and rubbed his eyes. The flashes were gone and for the time being he was able to see again. He didn't know how long that would last, though, so he slid under the covers and tried to fall asleep.

As he lay in the dark and desperately tried to get some rest, the previous week's events tumbled about in his mind.

Only days earlier he had comforted Brian in his office, offering to help him with the situation he was in. Then without warning Brian went crazy and showed up in Dallas's driveway and tried to kill him, or at least severely injure him.

Suddenly, Dallas recalled what Brian had said seconds before he pulled the trigger.

Not today.

He kept repeating it.

What did he mean?

To top everything off, earlier that morning Brian had sent him a book, *The Awakening.*

No matter how he tried, Dallas could not make sense of things. It all just seemed too random and out of character for Brian.

Somehow, he managed to fall asleep.

Sallad had hastily completed his other work for the week. He directed his attention back to his sequence. He wanted some way to have fun with his program.

A whimsical idea flashed before him.

Sallad decided he would make his sequence into a game and treat Dallas Easton as his game piece. As he thought about all the possibilities, he grew more and more excited. The possibilities were endless.

However, he needed to decide where to start.

Sallad sat behind his Interface and typed in an instruction that would cause Dallas to haphazardly fall down every time someone called him by name. In a sense, this was the equivalent to returning to the beginning of the game each time you committed a violation. Only the violation in this case was the word "Dallas."

Sallad laughed at the instruction he just sent. He

knew it was childish and didn't make any sense, but he needed something to run until he thought of more elaborate instructions.

And then it hit him.

Why not *really* screw with Dallas's mind?

Although Sallad was confident that life on Earth was precious, he conjured up the horrific idea of turning Dallas into a raging maniac.

A killer.

Sallad swiftly created an elaborate instruction that would imprint itself on Dallas and cause him to seek the demise of the closest person to him at random times.

Without hesitation, he transmitted the instruction.

Sallad left work early and headed down to the mall. Once there he took a carefree stroll through some of the spectacular shops.

He spent several hours at the mall, something he was not accustomed to, and all he had to show for it were three ice cream cones he had consumed.

The whole time he obsessed about Dallas.

When Sallad returned home he took a warm bath to relax himself. Although he continued to wonder what was happening hundreds of billions of light years away, he felt more relaxed than ever as he settled down on the sofa and fell asleep. Sweet dreams about his puppet on Earth awaited him.

Across the universe, Dallas Easton was waking up, a killer about to have one hell of a day.

CHAPTER 6

D allas was intermingled amongst the pedestrian traffic as he hurriedly walked along the busy thoroughfare. It was Sunday and he was headed to church.

He wasn't the most religious of individuals, but after the week he had just been through, he decided that a morning sermon seemed like the perfect elixir.

"Dallas," his coworker Tom spotted him among the amblers.

Without warning, Dallas suddenly crashed to the sidewalk as if he had been tripped. It took him a moment to comprehend what had just happened. He slowly got up and dusted himself off.

"Tom, uh, don't mind me. Obviously, I can't walk today," an embarrassed Dallas joked.

"Hey, no worries, it happens to the best of us. What are you doing out this way on a Sunday?"

"I decided to go to church today," Dallas said standing on the cathedral's concrete steps.

"Hey, well that's great, Dallas."

Dallas fell to the ground again.

"Dammit, what the hell is wrong with me?" Dallas grunted.

He tried to get to his feet but fell back down when Tom asked him if he was okay.

Tom extended his hand.

"Dallas, let me help you," but Dallas fell yet again.

This time he dragged Tom down with him.

Out of nowhere the sequence kicked in.

Suddenly, Dallas unleashed a fury of punches on Tom.

Confused, Tom tried to cover his face as his wife screamed in terror.

"Dallas, what the hell is wrong with you! I'm your friend. I'm trying to help you. Please, stop!"

Dallas just grew more infuriated. He bit Tom on the cheek and ripped from it a small piece of flesh. It was as if Dallas had instantly been inflicted with a form of human rabies.

Tom was no match for Dallas in this rage.

Dallas continued to assault Tom's midsection with heavy punches that caused blood to spurt from Tom's mouth.

Dallas grabbed him by the back of the neck and smashed his face into the concrete step. Tom wailed in excruciating pain. His wife jumped onto Dallas's back and swung wildly at his head. He shook her off his back, which caused her to roll down the steps to the sidewalk below where she fell unconscious.

In a final coup de grace, Dallas knelt down and grabbed Tom by the hair and smashed his skull into the pavement. Immediately, a dark, crimson pool of blood formed around Tom's head.

He was dead.

Dallas stood up.

Onlookers stared at him in disbelief and horror. Several of them screamed hysterically.

Dallas took off running down the block.

He had no idea what he had just done, unaware of his actions.

As Dallas scrambled through the maze of side streets to make his way back home, the sequence temporarily shut off.

Suddenly, Dallas was overcome with a sickening feeling as his mind comprehended the events that had just transpired.

More confusion set in.

He had just killed Tom.

It seemed as if he had no control over his actions.

And he was right.

The last thing he ever suspected was that he was

under the manipulation of some maniac from a distant galaxy. Why would he? The idea seemed preposterous.

Dallas burst through his front door and ran straight to the kitchen. He grabbed the book that Brian had sent him and frantically opened it to the first chapter, "The Unlocked Doors," and rifled through its pages.

He came to a quote atop the page.

"When the inner is imposed on the outer, then will man see himself as a beast."

Dallas dropped the book.

Was this a foreshadowing of what just happened?

What the hell did Brian know?

Where is he?

And where is the real Dallas Easton?

Sallad looked at the blinking monitor. A message scrolled across the screen and informed him that the control had just initiated a sequence into PowerDrive.

The revelation made him extremely happy.

"Excellent," he muttered to himself, "it worked. I'm a genius. He killed someone."

Sallad exluminated the previous instruction and intensified the newer one.

He looked at the clock.

The time had gotten away from him, and he was late for a meeting with Frederick Norsle, a leader in the field of Harnessing.

Sallad had reached out to Frederick earlier in the week and told him he had a new theory that he wanted him to review. Frederick knew Sallad's father and he was a very trustworthy associate.

It was Sallad's intention to confide in Frederick about the Awakening. He hoped to tap into Frederick's resources and expertise to "hypervate" the sequence onto himself, a process in which his thoughts, while in a subliminal state, would be able to manipulate Dallas Easton's life.

Sallad met Frederick at an elaborate restaurant at the Galleria in town. Frederick was a man of later years, roughly defined skin, medium build. As usual, he was dressed in a suit.

Sallad sat down and joined him.

"Hello, Sallad, always nice to see you're on time," Frederick remarked sarcastically.

"Sorry. I had to finish a few things at work."

"Well, you got me here, so now what?" Frederick was very direct.

"Why don't we order first."

After they had finished their meals and the table was cleared, Sallad was ready to share his recent discovery with Frederick.

"All right, Fred. I'm about to let you in on the biggest Harnessing breakthrough of the era."

Naturally, Frederick was a bit skeptical.

Norsle had worked in the field of Harnessing for quite some time and had seen several major discoveries throughout his career. His threshold for "breakthroughs" was extremely high. Needless to say, he was dubious of Sallad's claim. He certainly didn't expect Sallad to amaze him with anything revolutionary.

"What I'm about to tell you," Sallad continued, "is completely confidential and I trust you to keep it to yourself. Everything I am going to share with you has been diligently documented by me, and I assure you, it's completely real. Dare I say it is the biggest discovery we've seen in a long time."

"Dare you?" Frederick quipped.

Sallad reeked of confidence.

"Fred, I've been working extremely hard these past weeks on a new project that I call the Awakening. The Awakening is a computer sequence I've designed that will completely revolutionize Harnessing as we know it.

"About a month ago, I came across a defunct file on subliminal-hypotracing. It dealt with individuals who couldn't sleep, and how they could be helped."

"And how did you happen to come across this file? I thought you guys prided yourself on secrecy over there?" Norsle asked suspiciously.

"Well, that's the thing. Honestly, it was an accident. But I was so intrigued that I had no choice but to further explore it."

"No choice, huh?"

"I know some might think what I did was wrong, but just hear me out and I think you'll understand."

Sallad attempted to gauge Frederick's level of

interest, or even disapproval. But Norsle said nothing or showed no outward sign of any recognizable emotion. He simply sat stoic as he waited for Sallad to continue.

"Anyway, I began fooling around with this thing and got a spectacular idea. What if someone, given the right conditions, could actually subject their thoughts and ideas onto another individual? And in a sense control not only their subliminal, but their outward subliminal, their reality as well?"

Sallad again looked at Frederick, who still showed no signs of either intrigue or contempt.

"So fast forward several weeks. Through my creative ingenuity, I created an equilibrium sequence that could throw a control off balance, which I crossed with the subliminal sequence, to come up with what I call my Awakening sequence. After a few weeks of touchups with the expert technology we got over there, I was ready to try the sequence. I found the perfect control to use."

"And where did you find a complying control?" Frederick interrupted.

For the first time throughout their conversation, Sallad paused, not too eager to share the details.

Norsle was keen enough to discern Sallad's pause as somewhat ignoble.

"Well, there's kind of a catch there as well," Sallad started to explain.

"I figured," Frederick sardonically replied.

"I attained a being of Earth, named Dallas Easton,

and imposed upon him the Awakening sequence. And amazingly it worked!"

"Earth? Imposed? I'm not sure I want you to continue. I don't think I need to hear this. Not if I want to maintain my certification."

"Now wait a minute," Sallad interjected.

"No, you wait a minute. What you're telling me already has violated numerous Harnessing statutes. I'm not sure I want to hear any more."

"Trust me, Fred, you want me to continue," Sallad said with a wry grin.

"And how did you activate this thing?"

"To begin with," Sallad said, "I gave the Awakening a mind-frying file I created. After that, I began entering information into the computer through an intra-circuit wire. I connected a Kijyerty electrode to the machine to select a control. Basically, after that it was fairly easy."

"That's it?" Frederick asked.

"More or less. Of course, there was a tremendous amount of research and preparation, but with Epacseon's technology the connections were simple."

Sallad's tone grew more serious.

"Fred, you *must* believe me when I tell you how revolutionary this thing is. I mean, nothing like this has ever been tried. Nothing! I'm on the precipice of something spectacular!"

"And how do you know it works?" an incredulous

Norsle asked.

"That's the beauty of it. I entered a few little instructions. I had no idea if they would connect. But today I received a message on my Interface confirming the instructions were initiated into PowerDrive. It works!"

"And what were the instructions?"

"Well, it involves some physicality on the part of the subject, but no one is getting hurt from here. And it doesn't matter if the Earthlings are, this is new science. I can open up doors of technology that we thought to be unreachable. Do you have any idea what this means?"

By now Frederick Norsle's curiosity had been piqued. He knew that Sallad was in direct violation of the Harnessing Code, but he also knew that Sallad was right, and the Awakening could be something spectacular. He too was now entranced with the excitement surrounding the matter.

"And that is where I'm at, in a nutshell. But I see other possibilities, I'm just not sure of their potential. That, Fred, is why you are being let in on my secret. Together we can project subliminal consciousness onto others and take this sequence to the Awards."

The Awards honored the top scientists and their discoveries. They were the most prestigious event anywhere on the planet of Epacseon and were only held every ten years.

And in five months they would take place.

Anyone who received an Award was guaranteed

any career path they desired. But more importantly, they would go down in the annals of Epacseon lore.

"I'm still listening," Norsle said.

CHAPTER 7

Sallad and Frederick both had their heads buried in the numerous stacks of paper strewn across Sallad's kitchen table.

They had already been going over facts and theories for more than four hours. They had explored a multitude of different possibilities that would allow the sequence to be controlled strictly by Sallad's thoughts, rather than through computer-inputted instructions.

"Here is some stuff that might interest you," Sallad said, handing Frederick some papers.

Norsle examined the notes.

"No, what you need is a terminal cerebraldrive, and some good research. This stuff is good, but it is all premature. You've only had the sequence for a few days now, maybe it's not even working anymore."

"That's exactly why I need something I can control," Sallad interjected. "In order to make this thing a success, I need to know what is happening at all times. I can't be left in the dark hoping what I sent will connect. I need concrete..."

Frederick cut Sallad off, "Wait a minute, what if you were to...no, forget it, it's far too risky."

"No, what is it? Say it. If you're worried about me getting caught, that won't happen. Besides, all the hard stuff is done already. If anyone was going to suspect anything, they would have already noticed something by now," Sallad justified.

"Not for you getting caught," Norsle said, "but for you actually living his life through your dreams. It is possible, and I know what we can do, but you can really get trapped in the wrong subliminal. The consequences are disastrous. Forget I even said something."

"No. I'm not going to forget anything. What I have here is something so sacred. I need all the advances and insights I can get. I don't care if I get hurt, just as long as the sequence survives, and stays intact. And I'll have you for that. So tell me. Tell me now," Sallad stammered.

Frederick glanced at Sallad and then looked away.

He got up and nervously paced the room.

Frederick Norsle was a highly respected official in the field of Harnessing and could not afford to get caught up in Sallad's nefarious activities.

Still, he could not overlook what Sallad had

already accomplished. He had managed to develop a groundbreaking innovation, even if the ethics of it were questionable.

The Awakening was too enticing for Frederick to just walk away. Its science had already seduced him, and the project's potential had deeply embedded itself within Norsle.

However, if he wished to continue as a respected elder in the field of Harnessing, it was imperative that he walk away.

But he couldn't.

The Awakening contained far too much intrigue and mystique to pass up.

"There is a chance," Frederick started, "that if we use a terminal cerebraldrive as the conductor and replace the machine at your office with a facilitator, which was only to be used here at your home, that we could tap into your mental matter, brain waves and dreams, to operate the sequence."

Sallad jumped to his feet in excitement.

This was the very reason why he had consulted with Frederick-to tap into his profound expertise. Sallad could tell from Frederick's expression that he had just crossed the line and was willing to go the distance.

"Let's do it," Sallad said.

"There's a lot to be done."

"I don't care."

"A lot of responsibility and precautions."

"I'm ready."

"We could get caught. Fired. Expelled. And even worse," Frederick took a deep breath and slowly exhaled, his voice stern and tense, "Killed."

"I'm in," Sallad responded without hesitation.

Silence.

Sallad could almost hear the wheels as they grinded in his friend's mind.

A long pause, then...

"I'm in," Frederick Norsle said.

"All right then, it's settled," Sallad affirmed. "We're in this together. The Awakening is much more important than either of us. If one of us were to be discovered, we mustn't give up the other's identity. And, above all, we must promise to not reveal any information concerning the sequence, regardless of how small or inconsequential."

Frederick nodded in agreement.

Sallad extended his left hand.

Norsle stared at the hand for a few moments before he slowly extended his left hand.

Their hands clasped.

They were now one, along with the sequence.

"All right," Sallad grinned, "I'll decide when and where we meet since it is my sequence. And you will take care of the necessary set-up."

There was no objection from Frederick.

"I have the access to obtain any equipment we

need as long as I have a few days' notice," Sallad affirmed.

"Sallad, I hope you're right about this."

"Trust me," Sallad said.

CHAPTER 8

D allas placed the book Brian had sent him on his nightstand. He made his way downstairs to his kitchen to pour himself a drink. He did not drink often, but when he did drink, it was usually to excess.

Dallas grabbed a fifth of whiskey from a cabinet along with a small glass. He opened the freezer and tossed a few ice cubes into the glass. He proceeded to fill his glass about halfway with the brown liquor.

He stared at the glass for a moment before he lifted it to his lips, tilted back his head, and swallowed the alcohol.

The smeared grimace that had been across his face disappeared as he set the glass down on the table and poured himself another drink. This time he filled the entire glass.

He headed back upstairs to his room, bottle in one hand, glass in the other, and sat on the edge of his bed next to his nightstand.

Dallas flipped on the light and began to read his copy of *The Awakening*. This time, he started at the beginning.

A bevy of thoughts raced through his mind as he turned over page after page.

Where is Brian?

What's with this book?

Is Tom dead or was it a dream?

Maybe the whole thing was a dream?

By the time he was finished with the first chapter, he could not remember anything he had just read except the line about the mind being stronger than the present.

What the hell did that mean?

The mind, according to Peter von Hoffman, was a machine capable of erasing the present and creating a surreal reality.

Dallas, numb from the liquor, continued to drink anyway. He put the book down and rubbed his eyes. As he headed to the bathroom, he heard a faint bark.

Immediately, he spun around.

"Forrest, buddy," Dallas exclaimed as he walked over to the dog. "Where you bin, ol' pal? I missed ya."

There was no dog. Dallas was hallucinating.

He leaned down to pet Forrest and fell over on top of nothing.

"Where are ya? C'mere, boy. Wanna pet cha."

Dallas lay half comatose on the floor and his head whirled at a dizzying speed that made him grow nauseous. He tried to stand, but again tumbled to the floor. He reached for the corner of the desk, missed it, and knocked the nearly empty bottle of booze to the floor.

Eventually, he managed to stagger to his feet.

He desperately needed some fresh air.

Although wobbly, he grabbed the bottle and made it down the stairs and out the door. With no destination in mind, he began to walk down the street.

Dallas was drunk and swayed side to side as he plodded along the road. Occasionally, he stumbled and fell to the pavement, each time cursing at an invisible companion he blamed for tripping him.

He arrived at a busy intersection that did not look familiar to him. With no regard for oncoming traffic, he started to cross the street. Cars blared their horns as they whizzed by, one just barely missing him by a foot.

"You damn drunk, you're going to get yourself killed!" a passerby screamed out his window.

"Screw you," Dallas yelled back, "I's jest gonna take a wawk."

Not too far down the road, a police officer on patrol noticed the cars up ahead as they slammed on their brakes. It didn't take long for the cop to see the reason for the sudden commotion in front of him.

Dallas stood in the middle of the intersection and

screamed at the cars as they passed by in both directions.

"Screw y'all. I's am gonna fly. Ain't nothen wrong wit me. I dint killed nothen, I'd be home in bed readin what friend I shot me. All of this lie is killen us and no more for me who care."

The cruiser pulled up alongside Dallas. The cop opened his door and jumped out.

"All right, sir, stop right there and put the bottle down."

Dallas let the bottle fall from his hand, smashing into pieces as it hit the pavement.

"Now, get on your knees and place your hands behind your head."

"Occifer, I's Amercan, and ain't doin nothen but walken."

"Down on your knees, now," the cop screamed.

Dallas started towards the cop. The police officer pulled his gun and aimed it at Dallas.

"Put your hands up now. I'll blow you away dammit."

"Screw you too," Dallas said as he fell to the ground.

The cop bum rushed Dallas and violently grabbed his arm and twisted it behind his back. He then slapped a pair of cuffs on him, yanked Dallas to his feet, and threw him into the back of his car.

Dallas, now in custody, could hear the cop as he spoke on his radio.

"This is officer Corr, I have the 187 suspect in custody. Still wearing the same clothes matching the description from the church. I'm at Madison and Hunt, and bringing him in, 10-4."

Dallas closed his eyes and sobbed.

What is happening to me?

He had no control of anything anymore.

CHAPTER 9

Sallad programmed a number into his dialpager and pressed Send. A few moments later, a voice on the other end answered.

"Hello?"

"Frederick Norsle, please."

"May I ask who's paging?"

"Sallad."

"One moment."

Sallad was put on hold. It was the middle of the week, and in two days the sequence would have been activated for ten days. Sallad had a short amount of time to construct a facilitator.

A voice sounded on the other end.

"Sallad, how are you?"

"I'm okay, Fred, are you ready with the papers?"

"Yes, as a matter of fact I was finishing them up earlier today. Everything is set. The documents cover all the resources you will need to acquire, how to connect them, and what to start up."

Sallad smiled, "Excellent. Will you be ready this evening? I don't want to waste any more time."

"Yeah, I'll be ready. Your place at nine?"

"Yes. Oh, and Fred, transport me a copy of the machines so I can put in an order over here at work."

"Sallad, that's the beauty of it. I was wrong in my earlier assessment. Everything we need is at your home. We can have you hooked up by tomorrow evening."

"Just the news I needed to hear. See you tonight."

Sallad was ecstatic.

It was going to work. He would have complete control over his subject within a day's time.

Sallad faxed a copy of the Trenton report, a study he had just completed on the use of energy to create self-esteem, to Mr. Gere, his boss. The report was a bit lacking due to the amount of stress and anxiety Sallad had been under with the Awakening, but nonetheless it was thorough. Besides, Mr. Gere loved Sallad, and word had it that Sallad was up for a promotion.

He powered down the machines in his office, closed the door behind him, and headed for the elevator.

"Sallad," a voice called out.

It was Monte from down the hall.

Although in a hurry, Sallad reluctantly stopped.

"Hi, Monte, how are you?"

"Sallad, did you hear the news?" Monte asked eagerly with a smile splashed across his face.

"No, Monte, what's that?"

"Someone from this department is going to be getting promoted to Assistant Producer to help Mr. Gere."

"No kidding," Sallad smiled, knowing full well that he would be the one to help Gere with the productions of the corporation.

"I wonder who it is," Monte said with a gullible expression.

"Well, time will tell. See you later, Monte."

Sallad stepped into the elevator and headed for the Tram. A few moments later he arrived at his vehicle, got in, and set the destination for his home.

In less than a few hours, he and Frederick were going to send him into someone else's mind.

Sallad could hardly wait.

* * *

A groggy Dallas sat in the back of the police cruiser as he listened to the voices of two policemen outside the car. The cops discussed an arrest they made earlier on some guy.

Dallas felt tired.

He started to see a haze of thick clouds in front of him, and it hurt to keep his eyes open.

One of the cops banged on the side of the car and opened the door. He dragged Dallas, still in restraints, out of the car and threw him up against it.

"You're a real piece of work, mister," the cop said. "You caused a lot of trouble and problems this morning. You took another man's life."

Dallas blinked his eyes.

He wasn't dreaming, and the realization of what had happened earlier was beginning to make itself clear. Dallas suddenly felt queasy again.

Suddenly, without warning, the sequence once again activated itself and Dallas was consumed in a fit of hate and rage. He squared up with the officer and unleashed a powerful kick into the cop's groin, which immediately dropped him to the ground.

An incredible bout of strength overtook Dallas. Although handcuffed, he managed to jump on the fallen cop and deliver a fury of head butts square across the man's face. Blood spurted from his mouth and nose. The cop tried to grab his gun, but Dallas kicked it from his reach.

Dallas was relentless in his attack and refused to let up on the officer. The cop had already been beaten unconscious before his partner over near the station even realized what had transpired.

"Hey!" the other cop screamed.

He darted towards Dallas.

"What the hell are you doing?" he yelled as he

unholstered his side arm.

Dallas grabbed the gun on the ground near him and, although he was cuffed in the back, reached around his waist and squeezed off a shot. The bullet nipped the side of the cop's left leg and dropped him like a sack of bricks onto the cement.

Dallas scurried to the back of the squad car, squatted down, and grabbed the handcuff keys from the battered officer that lay next to him. He tried to unlock himself but could not maneuver his hands to properly fit the key into the keyhole. As he continued to struggle to unlock himself, a bullet ricocheted off the car's quarter panel, just missing Dallas.

"Drop the gun!" the cop screamed.

Other officers had heard the commotion and filed out of the station. Dallas was surrounded. He had no choice but to throw down the gun.

Immediately he was besieged by a gaggle of cops, who were quickly on top of him, their knees buried in his back. They cuffed his feet together and hogtied them to his hands.

A state of hysteria permeated the air.

Officer Corr, the cop that Dallas had shot, was carried into the police station. Dallas overheard the cops as they discussed Officer Ballock, the one he had beaten unconscious. He could hear them say that he was badly beaten and needed an ambulance to the hospital.

Inside the station, Dallas was thrown onto the

damp ground of a secluded holding cell. The cracked walls were a deep gray adorned in graffiti. The ceiling was old and falling apart, and the place stunk of grime, dirt, and stale beer.

Outside the cell, the agitated officers were talking.

"Man, this guy is really messed up in the head."

"No fooling. We better do something with him before he kills another person."

"We already got him for first-degree murder. We can also get him for battery of an officer, discharging a police-issued weapon upon another officer with intent to kill, endangerment of public, public disturbance and harassment, public intoxication, and some others."

"This dude ain't ever seeing the outside world again."

"He'll be lucky if he sees anything. He's going to the chair."

Dallas was passed out on the floor of the cell.

Even though he was still hogtied, they barricaded the outside of the cell and shut the lights off.

CHAPTER 10

Sallad knelt next to Frederick and helped him clear away the papers that were scattered across the rug.

"Listen," Frederick began, "we must work fast and efficiently, this could take some time and I don't want to be doing this in the morning when the Tullib recharges."

Sallad carried the paperwork over to the kitchen table. He grabbed the transfer wire and intra-circuit wire and went back into the living room.

Earlier that day, Frederick had called Sallad at work and instructed him to bring home the wires, even though he originally thought they wouldn't need anything extra.

"Where do you want these?" Sallad asked.

"Just put them down."

Norsle continued, "Do you realize what we are

doing? Maybe it hasn't hit me yet, which would explain why I'm actually going through with this, but we are in way deeper than we should be."

"Stop worrying," Sallad interjected. "Nothing will go wrong. Just tell me what we're going to do."

"All right. First, we need to be sure to establish a secure connection and hook up your telemonitor to the intra-circuit wire."

Norsle slid the telemonitor over to the middle of the room next to the comforchair and connected the wire to the input outlet on the back of the monitor.

"There. This wire will enable you to, at some point in time, actually see your control."

Frederick then inserted the telemonitor into the proper socket, grabbed the loose end of the wire, and connected it to Sallad's fax machine.

"Now, I'll need to disarm this fax machine of its transport wire and replace it with the transfer wire. This will enable the machine to convey your thoughts to Dallas, and vice versa."

Frederick plugged the fax machine into the back of the telemonitor. Then he disconnected Sallad's phone and set it on a table next to the chair.

Norsle scanned the equipment in front of him once again to ensure that everything had been properly connected. At this stage, even the slightest mistake could derail the entire project.

"Okay, what I need to do now," Frederick began,

"is program a number into your phone. When you have the phone plugged into your personal computer, which I will hook up later, you will have a number that you can dial to access you into the sequence. It's going to take a few hours to find the right number. Go get my papers I had with me."

Sallad quickly disappeared into the other room and retrieved the papers that Frederick needed, which had all types of technical mumbo-jumbo and various equations scribbled across them. Even Sallad, a man well-versed in Harnessing, barely comprehended most of it.

He handed the stack of notes to Frederick.

"Sallad, what is the office password you use to access the file?"

"What do you need that for?"

"Hey, listen, we're in this together. You want my help or not? Now give it to me."

It was not in Sallad's nature to easily trust everyone, perhaps because he was not exactly an ideal Epacseonite who could be trusted himself.

He let out a sigh and reluctantly said his password. "Dallas."

Norsle let out a small chuckle, obviously surprised by the simplicity of his colleague's password.

He jotted it down.

"Did you have any other words or codes needed to access the Awakening?"

Again, Sallad showed reluctance.

"Yes. Before any instruction can be submitted, a specific code number must be programmed. It's the numerical version of the code word," Sallad explained.

"I don't have time to figure it out, now tell me."

Sallad easily sensed Frederick was uneasy and beginning to get impatient and nervous.

The last thing he needed was for Norsle to get cold feet and have a change of heart about helping him.

"412219," Sallad recited. "Listen, Fred, that number must not be used to access the file, or else it will destroy it. It can only be used to create and send instructions. That is critically important. You got that?"

Sallad was stern in stating the importance of using the code word. If used improperly, the Awakening would be destroyed.

"I hear you," Frederick responded. "Why don't you go pick up some food. It will give me some time to finish all the finer details that need to be completed. Oh, and pick up some fuzzwire and a metal ring, the kind used in electric vacuums. I should be ready for them when you get back."

Sallad was intrigued, "What are those for?"

"Because I'm hungry," Norsle joked.

"I'm serious."

"So am I. Wait until you're back. I think you'll be surprised. And quite pleased, I might add."

Sallad left for the food and supplies.

Frederick buried his head in his papers and got

back to work, ensuring that everything would be ready in preparation for the beta test.

He worked diligently for almost an hour. He checked and rechecked every connection that had been established between the wires, telescreen, and fax machine.

Once he was confident that everything had been properly connected, he turned his attention to configuring Sallad's computer. This task required him to design a code that would allow Sallad to access his office Interface from the private confines of his living room.

After everything had been completed, it was time for the final phase. Frederick grabbed one of the transfer wire's loose ends and insulated it in poly-rich plastic. This end would be the key in transmitting instructions.

He then punched in Sallad's password and called up the Awakening sequence. He paid extra attention to make sure he did not use the number to activate or register the sequence as Sallad had instructed.

The sequence successfully loaded and illuminated the monitor with its thousands of bytes of data.

Frederick retrieved the paperwork he had worked on at his office and copied the information, verbatim, into the computer's mainframe.

He still was not finished by the time Sallad got back, almost two hours later.

"Fred, I hope this fuzzwire is important, I went to three different places to find it."

"Thanks, set it over there."

Norsle hardly paid any attention to Sallad, as he was too engrossed in programming the new database.

His program complete, he pressed a series of keys to properly route the data to the proper directories, while at the same time saving the new information.

Confident everything was properly and securely stored, he powered down the machine and wheeled his chair over next to the comforchair where the telemonitor and fax machine were already hooked up and ready to go.

"Let's eat, I'm starving," Frederick said, looking at the Gredatian food and chips Sallad had bought.

As they ate, Frederick explained the need for the fuzzwire and metal ring.

The metal ring would be used to create a headring that would be fitted around the circumference of Sallad's skull. The fuzzwire would be intertwined through the hollow core of the ring.

The fuzzwire had three separate ends. Two of its ends were attached to small electrodes that would be positioned and affixed just above Sallad's temples. The remaining end would be plugged into a port on the transfer wire. Both ends of the transfer wire would be plugged into the intra-circuit wire, which connected the other machines.

The copper-like material of the headring would also serve as an added level of conductivity, which would ensure efficient and maximum transfer of electricity through the entire apparatus, thus creating an interstellar highway for Sallad's dreams to travel into Dallas's mind.

With all this complete, Sallad, lying comfortably in the comforchair, would be able to access the sequence on his computer, and through its connection with the telemonitor, would have the ability to see the sequence being run. Due to Frederick's ingenious design, whatever Sallad dreamt while adorned with the headring would be conveyed directly into Dallas Easton's brain circuitry.

Simply put, it was all just a matter of the transfer of electricity. The power of Harnessing was limitless.

Sallad barely touched his food, even though Gredation was his favorite. He was too enthralled with what Frederick Norsle had to say.

Although everything was operable, Frederick was hesitant to initialize a test. He informed Sallad he wanted to wait and give the various machines time to store up enough energy. However, he was extremely confident that soon enough the dream machine would be ready for use.

It was the wee hours of morning.

Sallad put a pot of Gotcha on the stovetop.

In a few short hours, he would put on much more. He would don a headring that would allow him to effectively control the dreams and actions of another individual.

However, there was one important and limiting stipulation to employing the machine.

It could only be used when Easton was awake.

Norsle had researched the time difference, and the idea didn't seem so preposterous. Earth was thirteen hours ahead of Epacseon. Frederick devised a schedule that allowed for Sallad to run the Awakening from 7 a.m. to 10 p.m. Earth time. This dictated that Sallad would have to sleep from 6 p.m. to 9 a.m. Epacseon time.

Thus, when Dallas was sleeping, Sallad would be awake. When Sallad was asleep and in the dream mode, Dallas would be awake.

Sallad was unconcerned with the possibility that the time difference would pose an issue that required him to spend ample time away from the office. Because he was so well respected at Aspirion, he could simply readjust his work schedule.

Besides, he honestly couldn't care less if his work was affected. He was hours away from the most significant Harnessing breakthrough in Epacseon's history.

The pair went to work on the final details.

CHAPTER 11

The florescent lighting flickered above Dallas and woke him from his prickly slumber. Its constant low din had been his cellmate throughout the night. The cell's damp, cracked cement floor was a far cry from his safe and comfortable bed.

An overweight prison guard, chomping on a stale cigar, clanged open the rusty bar doors and threw a towel and a pair of blue trousers at him.

"All right," said the guard, "you got twenty minutes to shit, shower, shampoo, shine, and shave. After you're cleaned up you can make a phone call."

Dallas made little effort to get to his feet.

"Let me warn you now. I'm down from Ironwood Prison. Already got state's permission for an expedited transport," the grumpy corrections officer stated.

"And since you been deemed some kinda threat, there ain't nothing anyone's gonna do to stop it. Now hurry it up, you got nineteen minutes left."

Dallas gathered up the clothes off the floor and plodded towards the shower area. Still dumbfounded by the previous day's events, he was in no real hurry to get anywhere.

At present, he felt suicidal, still unaware of his condition. In his mind, he thought he had transformed into a monster, oblivious to the fact that he was indeed someone else's monster.

Over the past few days his best friend had sent him an odd book with no explanation, and then tried to kill him, also for no apparent reason; he had viciously murdered Tom; he had severely injured a police officer while restrained; he could not control his balance; and his dog had run away.

Perhaps Forrest had sensed what was about to befall Dallas and had tried to get as far away from him as possible.

What on earth went wrong?

Dallas made a promise to himself that as soon as the chance presented itself, he would take his own life. He didn't care how, but he refused to go on living a life in which he had no control over his thoughts and actions.

He sobbed uncontrollably as he showered.

After he was dressed, he was again restrained and ushered into a small, dank room that had a mirror on the wall and a phone on the center table.

"You got a half hour," the cop said and left.

He walked around the corner and entered a room where several other cops were huddled. They all watched Dallas through the two-way mirror.

"What do you think?" the cop asked the detective.

"I don't get it. I know this guy. I mean I don't know him personally, but I've seen him over at Herzig and Statton, where Bob works. He was a great guy, so everyone said. Always upbeat, at least when I saw him. I just don't get it."

"Go figure," another officer said.

Dallas sat at the table and stared at himself in the mirror. He looked like a different version of the Dallas Easton he knew. Although he had just showered, his eyes were dark and baggy, his hair disheveled, and he sported a 5 o'clock shadow.

He looked at the phone.

Who the hell am I going to call?

His parents were dead. He had no siblings. Didn't have any close friends, other than Brian. And he was too embarrassed to call one of the partners at his firm.

Dallas had always been his own man, and now he was his own enemy.

He picked up the black phone and slowly dialed a number. The phone rang for about a minute, until a sullen voice answered.

"Hello?" the voice said.

"Brian? It's Dallas," there was a long pause. "Brian, are you there?"

"Dallas. Why are you calling me?"

"It's a long story. Brian, I don't know what's going on. I don't know who I am anymore, what I've done. I don't even know what day it is, or what time it is."

"I thought you were dead, Dallas."

"Brian," Dallas took a deep breath, "did you try to kill me?"

"Dallas, I only did what I felt was right."

"Wait a minute. I was hoping that I was dreaming, and you were going to say you didn't know what the hell I was talking about. But I guess I don't care. Everything is happening too fast and too strange to comprehend. Brian, last Saturday, whenever the hell that was, you came over to my house and tried to kill me."

Dallas grew irate, "Brian, you son of a bitch, you tried to kill me! What the hell's wrong with you!"

"What's wrong with me? Dallas, what on earth are you doing with yourself? I haven't heard from you in five days. Where have you been? What are you talking about? And where are you?"

"I'm in jail." Dallas felt a lump grow in his throat. "Brian, I killed Tom and tried to go after a cop."

"Wait a minute," Brian was confused and had no idea what his friend was talking about, "you're in jail? You killed Tom? Tom from work?"

"Yes, dammit."

"Dallas, I have no idea what you're talking about. I have been trying to find a job these past few days. Where are you, downtown? I'm coming down."

"Brian," Dallas was extremely confused and on the verge of going crazy, "I am not Dallas Easton anymore. I don't know who I am. I'm being transferred to Ironwood within the hour."

"Dallas, that place is hell. You've heard the stories. They can't move you until they talk to your lawyer."

Dallas heaved, "I don't have one."

"I'm bringing mine. I'll be there as soon as I can."

"Whatever," Dallas chuckled.

He was losing his mind.

He hung up the phone.

"Somebody want to tell me what he was just talking about?" Detective Brady queried the room.

"I have no clue. But the guy is messed up. Give him a blood test," he said, looking at another officer.

A few minutes later an officer opened the door. He was accompanied by two other cops, who each had a pair of cuffs ready to place on him.

Suddenly, without reason, Dallas felt queasy.

The sequence activated itself once again.

Dallas charged the lead cop and smashed his face into the brick wall. The loud and unpleasant sound of cheekbones breaking could be heard as the cop slid to the floor, his face smearing a red streak down the wall.

The other two cops charged Dallas and knocked him to the ground. More officers stormed into the room.

A gunshot went off.

One of the cops accidentally shot himself in the foot as he reached for his gun. He thrashed on the floor in pain.

It took four officers to restrain Dallas. He laughed hysterically as they wrestled with him. Finally, they were able to hogtie his hands and feet together. The prison guard from Ironwood secured an extra set of shackles around him just to be safe.

An orderly, who had accompanied the Ironwood guard, ran in with a sedative-filled syringe. The cops restrained Dallas, who was still laughing hysterically, as the nurse jammed the needle into his arm.

A few moments later he was asleep.

Everyone exited the room and left Dallas alone and unconscious on the concrete floor.

The chief of the department had heard the melee and demanded an explanation from the officers who were present. The chief, a gruff man whose presence filled the room, wanted to know just how Easton could cause so many problems, all while under the supervision of a bevy of cops.

No one had an explanation.

The Ironwood guard suggested to the chief that they load Dallas into the transport vehicle while he was unconscious.

"S'pose it'll take an hour or so to transport him. He'll get processed and then we'll be in touch. Won't be your problem no more," the corrections officer stated.

"Good, do it," the chief stammered.

Detective Brady chimed in, "Sir, are you sure he has consulted a lawyer, and permission has been granted to dismiss him from this precinct?"

The chief swallowed some water from a half-crushed paper cup he held, coughed a bit, and smiled, "He's been cleared to leave."

"All right," the guard replied, "I need two of your men to accompany me. Regulations and shit."

"That son of a bitch has already injured three of my men and I can't spare any others. I still have the city to protect."

"Duly noted. But can't move him without credible company. We won't be gone for more than three hours."

"Dammit," the chief moaned. "Murphy, grab your partner and accompany them to Ironwood."

Outside the station, a red Mercedes careened into the parking lot. Two men quickly exited the vehicle. One was Brian. The other was his lawyer, Stephen Kern. They hastily proceeded into the station.

"Yes?" the female desk clerk asked.

"A man, Dallas Easton, was brought in here today. He has been neglected counsel as of this point. We demand to see him."

"Excuse me, Brian," Stephen chimed in. "Ma'am,

I am the representation for Dallas Easton. I work with my client at the law firm of Herzig and Statton. He is not yet certified, and that is why I am here to aid in counsel. We would like to speak with him. We have that right."

The lady behind the desk was unsure what to do, so she called the chief over.

"I'm Chief Robbins, what can I do you gents for?"

"I'm Stephen Kern, Dallas Easton's lawyer. I'd like to see him."

"Well, sir, I'm afraid that's not possible. Right now Mr. Easton is under an anesthesia that was given to him to sedate him."

"What! You have no bounds in which to instruct such a procedure. You are in consequence of violating his civil rights."

"Well, now hold on a minute, sir. Your client has brutally assaulted several of my men, after having already shot and wounded two others. The man was out of control and had to be reprimanded. As far as his civil rights go, he's in cuffs now awaiting transport to Ironwood."

"This is preposterous," Kern shouted, "you have no right to transport him. And second, was he given the anesthesia before or after he was placed in cuffs?"

"Before," the chief lied, knowing he had in fact violated Dallas's civil rights. But the man was a threat and had to be contained.

"I demand to see him. You have no right to move him, until he has spoken with counsel and is advised by

Scott W. Fedor

me as of what to do. Furthermore, as I understand, no charges have been filed against him, and if you choose to do so, he has the right to make his statement. Now I demand to see him."

The chief was well beyond irritated.

He hated lawyers.

He knew he overstepped his bounds, but he was fed up with Easton and wanted to rid himself of him as soon as possible. Let the courts sort it out.

"Well, he's sedated right now. Why don't you gentlemen step into my office. Let me get you a cup of coffee and I can brief you on the whole situation" the chief said, feigning appeasement.

"No," Kern stammered, "as Mr. Easton's attorney I must have him present and awake before any statements are given."

The chief pointed to a row of cheap plastic chairs permanently fixed to the wall, "Well then, have a seat and wait."

Stephen and Brian took a seat.

A few minutes later, the Ironwood guard moseyed on into the lobby and explained the current situation in a carefree manner.

Stephen was very stubborn and continued to insist that Dallas had to be conscious before any further steps, whatever they may be, could be taken.

One of the cops handed the chief some smelling salts. They carefully guarded Dallas while the chief waived the salts back and forth under Easton's nose.

A few minutes later, Dallas was awake and groggy.

He sat at a table, in cuffs, and drank coffee as Kern explained the situation in detail to him. He was adamant that Dallas not say another word to anyone other than Kern until the arraignment, which would take place the following day.

The chief grudgingly agreed not to transport Dallas until after the arraignment. He would remain at the city jail until the following morning.

After Brian and Stephen left, Dallas was once again returned to his cell and locked up.

Everyone at the station returned to work and their lives resumed as usual. Except for Dallas.

He had no idea whose life he was living anymore.

CHAPTER 12

allad took his time as he meticulously intertwined the fuzzwire and transfer wires. This was a critical step in the entire process. He could not afford any mishaps.

He connected one end of the transfer wire to the intra-circuit wire, whose other ends were linked between the computer and fax machine.

Frederick powered up the various machines. He then took a seat in the comforchair and excitedly pecked away at the keyboard as he inputted the code to call up the mind-frying sequence and access the Awakening.

The sequence filled the screen with numerous rows and columns of data bytes that indicated all systems were go and ready to be initiated.

Once Sallad touched the homing bar, the

sequence would be activated.

Sallad was eager to begin.

"It's three in the morning," Norsle said. "You have about six hours to try to launch something. You ready?"

"More than ready," Sallad responded.

"All right. Place the ring around your head and fasten it tight. Pull all the machines within arms' reach and position the keyboard in front of you on your lap. After you confirm activation for the program I installed, you just need to fall asleep. Whatever you dream will transpire on Earth, at least that is the intention. You'll be able to see everything once we get the telemonitor hooked up."

"What's the program?" Sallad asked.

"Type the letters W-A-K-E-U-P, and the number 593165. Now press the homing bar twice."

Sallad pressed the bar twice.

"You're all set, sweet dreams."

Sallad closed his eyes and began to fall asleep.

One of the advantages to the headring was that the electrodes in the fuzzwire helped induce somnia quicker than if naturally trying to fall asleep.

Frederick went to the kitchen to pour himself a cup of Gotcha. He decided to remain at Sallad's until he awoke in the event there was a malfunction or other issue that needed to be addressed.

Immediately, Sallad's mind was filled with giant purple spots that zipped past his eyes and bombarded off imaginary black walls.

He had already reached REM state and his mind was now engulfed in blackness, except for the purple spots that careened every which way.

Sallad was being mentally transported through the transfer wire to Earth.

Everything went white.

Moments later, a handcuffed figure slumped in a chair began to materialize.

It was Dallas.

Inside the room, three men were talking as they stood in front of Dallas.

"On your feet," one of the men demanded.

Seconds later, Dallas was seated on a bench in the holding area of the prison transport vehicle en route to the courthouse, with two of the men.

Although Frederick had established a timetable in which to conduct the experiment, unbeknownst to either of them, the construct of time did not exist while Sallad was inside the sequence.

Because the brain waves generated in his dreams controlled the sequence and status of life on Earth, he also controlled its time. Simultaneously, while he controlled the time on Earth, Epacseon existed within a vacuum state of four-dimensional time, and, thus, by default he also controlled its time.

Sallad was in over his head with this experiment.

Unbeknownst to him, this cessation of linear time

progression would eventually cause both planets to cross times, and thus destroy a balanced solar system.

Dallas stood before the judge.

He was arraigned on a bond of $250,000 and was free to go until his trial four days later.

Sallad's subconscious grew frustrated with the events that were transpiring and he concentrated harder.

He dreamt that Dallas escaped into the parking lot searching for a getaway vehicle. He visualized Dallas as he picked up a brick and smashed the window of a black Oldsmobile. He jumped in the car and tried to start it when he heard a voice.

"Dallas, what are you doing, man? You just got bailed out. Are you crazy or something?" Brian screamed at him as he stood next to Stephen.

Dallas looked around.

"Brian, what did I just do?"

"I don't know, man, but you're screwed up."

Dallas sprung from the car and attacked Brian.

Under Sallad's control, Dallas was invincible.

He grabbed Brian by the back of the neck and hurled his face into the car's bumper. Brian was instantly knocked out and now lay on the ground.

Dallas immediately turned his sights on Stephen and chased him across the lot. Once he caught him, he wrestled him to the ground and started to beat him furiously while ripping out clumps of his hair.

An elderly couple heard Stephen's screams and

saw the two men fighting. They quickly scurried into the courthouse and yelled for the police.

Three cops stormed out of the building and saw the fracas. They all gang tackled Dallas to the ground.

"You're the psycho who just made bail, you crazy bum," one of the cops yelled.

Dallas easily broke free of their restraint and in one fell swoop simultaneously kicked two of them with a sweeping roundhouse kick.

He had never taken a karate lesson in his life.

But then again, this wasn't his life anymore.

He spun around and charged at the other cop, knocking him to the ground. As the two wrestled on the ground, Dallas managed to grab the officer's firearm and squeeze off a shot.

Easton jumped to his feet and fired two more shots at the other cops. In a matter of seconds, Dallas Easton had just murdered three police officers.

He slowly ambled over to Stephen, who was crawling across the pavement, and stood over him.

"You're crazy, man. I try to help you and this is what you do!" a terrified Stephen screamed.

Dallas pointed the gun at Stephen.

"Bang, you're dead," he said mockingly as he pretended to shoot him.

Kern continued to crawl across the concrete parking lot, but regardless of how fast he scrambled, Dallas kept pace, pointing the gun, and taunting him.

"Help! Somebody! Please!" Kern screamed.

Sallad was getting bored with the charades and amped up the action in his mind.

Dallas stepped in front of Stephen. He stared deep into his eyes, then aimed the gun at the lawyer's left leg and fired three times. Kern erupted with a shrieking cry of agony that permeated the air.

Innocent bystanders scattered, running amok as they tried to flee from the madman that Dallas had become. Two patrol cars, sirens blaring, careened into the parking lot. Dallas lifted the barrel of the gun inches from Stephen's face.

"You piece of trash," Dallas remarked.

He gingerly squeezed the trigger.

Three different cops were in a prime position to take down Dallas. They called for him to stop, but he turned and fired at them. Instantly, a barrage of bullets filled the air, whizzing across the tops of the cars and ricocheting in several directions. Miraculously, all their bullets somehow managed to miss Dallas.

Dallas sprinted into the middle of the road. An oncoming car furiously beeped as it approached him.

Easton took direct aim at the female driver.

She slammed on the brakes and grinded to a screeching halt. Dallas, under the manipulation of Sallad, fired off a shot into the vehicle's windshield, striking the woman and instantly killing her.

He walked to the driver's side door, opened it,

and shoved her slumped body onto the thoroughfare.

All the while, bullets continued to miss him.

By now, the streets were filled with panic and horror. People screamed as they ran every which way in search of cover. It was impossible for the officers to get a clear shot due to all the commotion.

Dallas hopped into the woman's car, slammed the door shut, and sped away. The police opened fire, but their shots just bounced off the tail end of the car.

They were unable to stop him as he drove off.

Dallas had no idea where he was going.

Sallad had control over every aspect of Dallas's life. Dallas could not clearly comprehend what had happened. He realized he was speeding away from a scene where he had just inflicted a great deal of mass chaos and savagely murdered several people, but he wasn't able to rationalize the reason for his doing so.

The Awakening had complete control.

Dallas rounded a corner at such a high rate of speed that the car listed a few inches off the ground. He quickly veered onto a side street and then zigzagged onto another street. For the time being, he had successfully evaded the pursuit and broken free from the mayhem.

Dallas slowed the vehicle to the side of the road, hopped out, and proceeded to run down the street. He had no idea where he was going; neither did Sallad. All Easton knew was that he had to continue to run.

How fast or how far he ran, or how much energy

he continued to exert, was inconsequential.

Under the sequence's spell, Sallad did not feel any effect or grow tired. Neither did his control subject.

Dallas's path soon arrived at an old, dilapidated, and abandoned warehouse. He scanned his surroundings and then quickly ducked into the decrepit shelter.

He had covered so much distance that he had no idea where he even was. Judging by the surroundings, he was not in the most desirable part of town. Several of the properties were in shambles, looking as if the next wave of severe weather would cause them to crumble. The burned-out and rusted frames of ransacked cars littered the street on both sides. Trash was strewn everywhere.

Dallas kicked aside the clutter in front of him as he traversed his way through the decaying warehouse.

Brief moments of lucidity would come and go, each only lasting a fraction of a second. It was during these moments that he felt exhausted, although any attempt at sleep would be futile. He was cognizant of the fact that his body would not allow it.

Whenever he experienced the slightest urge to stop and attempt to rest, some inner force compelled him to continue wandering through the dingy building.

He came to a set of stairs that he followed down into a dark recess. Dallas pressed his hands firmly against the cracked stone walls to guide him through the darkness.

Upon reaching the base of the stairs, he slowly continued to trudge through the passageway. Once he reached the bottom of the stairs, he cautiously continued through the murky and narrow corridor. The smell of urine wafted throughout the halls with its repugnant scent.

Suddenly, a series of tremors coursed throughout Dallas's entire body.

Sallad twitched. Frederick was shaking him.

"Sallad, come on. Sallad, time's up."

Sallad jolted awake and opened his eyes.

"Huh? Fred, my word, is that you?

"Of course it's me."

"Fred! It worked! It's amazing! I could see him! I could really see him! I could see everything!"

Sallad could barely contain his excitement. He began enthusiastically telling Frederick what he had just experienced. He rambled so fast that Norsle had to keep telling him to slow down.

It was 7 a.m. and there were still two more hours in which the machine could be used. However, Frederick had woken Sallad prematurely to check in on how things were progressing.

"You mean you could actually see the guy?" Frederick asked, stunned.

"Yes! I could see everything! Everything! I could control it all! It's as if, as if I was right there beside him! We don't need the telemonitor!" Sallad exclaimed. "I didn't care what I did! The only thing I cared about was that it was me doing it! Me! Fred, my friend, we have found a way to control the guy's life! He's gone absolutely mad!

His entire existence is under my control!"

Sallad let out a maniacal laugh, "Chaos and violence are entertaining to watch, but it's even more fascinating when you direct it! We must tell the Awards about this immediately!"

"No," Frederick interjected. "It's not ready yet. We must proceed with caution. There is more that we need to understand."

"There's nothing more to understand, it works!"

"Sallad, this thing is still unstable. For instance, we don't know what's happening right now. We don't know the effect the sequence has on its subject. These are things we won't know until we have conducted multiple experiments."

"Fine. I'm going back in right now."

"No. You have to go to work. It's imperative to keep up appearances," Frederick cautioned.

"But I need to know what's happening there right now. I just left the guy alone in a building. What if someone finds him? I need to go back!"

"No, Sallad! We must adhere to the time construct and its implied rules. If I had to venture a guess, I would suspect that he is right where you left him, just of his own free will. And it's important that he remain in control until we hook you up and send you back in. Tonight at 6 p.m. when the schedule deems it."

Sallad smirked.

It was apparent to him that Frederick was enjoying

this as much as he was. And he needed Norsle. At least until all the technical work was completed and proven to be stable, repeatable, and sustainable.

Once that critical milestone was achieved, Sallad would be able to cut Frederick out of the deal. The fame, power, prestige, and especially the Awards, would be his, and his alone.

"Listen, Sallad, right now that guy has the ability to control his own life. He is going to discover what he did. But he won't know why. Tonight, when you go back in, you must be extremely careful. Any clues you give off while sleeping will disassociate you from his subliminal. In other words, they will tip you off and will have the potential to alert him that something is wrong."

Sallad was confused.

This was why he still needed Frederick.

"What do you mean?" he asked.

"Well, you must not dream or conjure up any references to Epacseon, yourself, me, this machine, anything. You need to keep our two worlds separate."

It was plain to see how serious Frederick was.

"Bottom line is that you must not place the control in any situation in which it is a foreigner. You can play your little mind games, torment him, whatever," Frederick continued, "although I feel it would be more apt to use the sequence for something more constructive.

But you must never disclose in any fashion the notion that something else might be controlling him. The consequences could be devastating."

His comment lingered in the air for a moment.

"What consequences? He can't touch us."

"Just be smart with this thing, Sallad. Don't try getting too fancy. Not yet. Not until we can confirm the sequence is stable."

"Yeah, yeah, I hear you."

"I'm serious about this," Norsle was even more stern as he reiterated his warning. "The consequences could be devastating."

"Okay. Okay."

"I need to get to work. I'll see you tonight," Norsle said and left for work.

Sallad peered over at the comforchair and bank of machines. He didn't put too much stock into most of what Frederick had to say.

This was Sallad's sequence.

He had invented it.

And as far as he was concerned, it was his to do with as he pleased.

He still had a lot intended for Dallas Easton.

CHAPTER 13

Dallas slowly opened his eyes. It felt as if a stack of quarters weighed down each eyelid. His entire body ached, devoid of any verve, as if he had just run a marathon while wearing a suit made of bricks.

How was he to know that a side effect of the sequence was the energy it extracted from its subjects? It was only once someone had been released from its grip that the full toll could be felt.

He had lost all concept of time and had no idea how long he had been asleep. After doing his best to rub away the sleep from his eyes, he surveyed the scene around him.

Where the hell am I?

Dallas took a few moments and tried to collect his

thoughts. A fog had also seemed to envelop his brain.

Finally, he gradually began to remember bits and pieces of the preceding few days. At present, the last thing he recalled was being arraigned at the courthouse with Brian and Stephen.

The full picture of what had transpired over the previous hours suddenly flashed in his mind. The events that had unfolded quickly surfaced as if they had just happened seconds earlier.

Unfortunately for Sallad, he had no idea that a major drawback of the sequence was that Dallas would have the ability to recollect events as vividly as Sallad did once the session was terminated.

Dallas was overcome with a revolting feeling.

What have I done!

He leaned over and threw up. For the next several minutes he sat still in the dark passageway and sobbed as he recalled his abhorrent actions.

After he had emptied himself of tears, he heaved a sigh and tightened his muscles. He tried to stand but had no strength, still too weak from the kinetic energy used up while he was under control of the Awakening.

His transgressions continued to flood his memory bank, causing him to vomit once more.

Dallas Easton was scared to death.

What is happening?

Try as he may, he would never be able to explain any of this. No matter what he could say or do, no one of sound mind would believe him.

He couldn't even believe it himself.

The haunting and familiar thoughts of suicide he wrestled with while in jail resurfaced and tormented him. However, he refused to take that route. He had always considered himself a fighter, someone who rallied when the chips were down. He vowed he would not kill himself.

At least for the time being.

But how could he rationalize things?

Something had to have control of him. It was the only logical explanation. But he had no idea what on earth it could be. He just had an eerie feeling that some unknown force was at play.

The last thing he would ever suspect was that his condition was attributable to a celestial deviant halfway across the galaxy with a strip of copper wrapped around his head.

What he did know, though, was that he couldn't stay where he was. He had to find a more secure location until he could devise some course of action.

The damp and dark dungeon he currently found himself in had been a good spot to rest, but he knew it wouldn't take long for the police to scour the city and discover his location. For all he knew, they could be outside right now, waiting to mow him down as soon as he emerged from his current confines.

But they weren't.

Dallas finally made his way to his feet but had to

use the wall for support.

As he exited the building, he needed to shield his eyes from the afternoon sun that hovered above and shined down brightly.

He must've slept longer than he thought.

Great. Where am I going to go in the daylight?

The police were out cruising for him. The news had plastered his face on every station and alerted the citizens to be on the lookout. And he didn't exactly know where he was in location to any familiar landmarks.

Fortunately, the city was of decent size. Dallas could probably get lost for a few hours, but he wasn't sure if he could risk it. He wasn't exactly a model citizen who could easily blend in.

Mr. Easton was a crazed lunatic killer.

Obviously, retreating to his home was out of the question. That was the first place that law enforcement would scope out. Besides, he didn't really need anything, except money. But he had his wallet. Still, he couldn't take the risk of going to a bank without being caught.

He could run.

That's it!

He would make his way crisscrossing the country, only stopping in obscure towns, and never for more than a day. He would get his meals from dumpsters until he was far enough away from the city in more unknown locales.

Then he could earn petty cash doing odds and

ends for people he came across. He would adopt a frugal lifestyle.

Yes! It could work, he told himself.

But being forced to choose that lifestyle isn't fair!

Dallas had worked hard to establish his lot in life. He refused to cower in the shadows like some deranged madman who was guilty of all the violence and murder.

But he was guilty.

He was guilty of everything.

Whether it was true that he was being controlled, it was still Dallas who had committed all the heinous acts.

Easton had a severe conscience problem.

He knew the right thing to do was to surrender to the authorities and turn himself in. But he also knew that he wasn't entirely at fault.

There was only one thing to do.

Dallas Easton had to figure out what had possessed him and compelled him to hurt all those innocent people.

He realized that he must figure out what was controlling him before it caused him to hurt others. But where was he going to go? One thing was for sure, he had to go somewhere.

Sallad had turned him into a deranged beast and stripped away his ability to reason while under control of the Awakening.

When in its grasp, he was no longer Dallas Easton.

He was a sick, twisted, ruthless savage who had

killed several people and was bound to do so again.

Dallas fished a ragged hat out of a nearby dumpster, put it on, and proceeded to hail a taxi. Luckily, he was in a part of town where it was commonplace for people to keep their heads down and stay to themselves.

The driver took him to the city library.

No one paid any notice as he entered through the door and proceeded to the men's room. He found an empty stall situated the farthest from the door.

Dallas sat down to collect his thoughts.

Although he felt safe for the time being, what was he going to do? He couldn't spend the rest of his life locked in bathrooms attempting to conceal himself.

Something was controlling him.

There has to be.

Dallas remained in the restroom for several hours. The dwindling foot traffic that came in and out indicated it was getting late.

It was time to leave.

He exited the stall and splashed some water on his face. The mirror's reflection that stared back at him was no longer that of an attractive, young legal aid full of vitality. What Easton saw when he looked at himself was a disoriented and sloppy killer.

His handsome face was tired and worn. His clothes were wrinkled and reeked of filth. He resembled one of the poor souls he used to step over and ignore when he walked the city streets to some fancy restaurant on his lunch break.

Dallas left the bathroom and moved at just swift enough of a pace so as not to draw any unwanted attention.

The massive clock, adorned with thick Roman numerals, that hung high on the library's wall indicated it was almost 5 p.m. The library closed in a few minutes.

Dallas was hungry.

He couldn't remember the last time that he had eaten something. Still wearing the hat, he stepped out of the confines of the library and onto the busy rush-hour sidewalk. Dallas walked with the pace of the other pedestrians and kept his head down, doing his best to blend in with the evening crowd.

He turned a corner and disappeared down an empty alley. Easton hurried through the littered alley, with only a handful of hobos slouched against the dirty brick walls for company.

The rain had started to come down stronger, and as Dallas stopped to rest along the building's exterior, he spied three bums huddled together under a rain-drenched cardboard box.

They eyed Dallas, thinking he was one of them.

CHAPTER 14

Dallas had no idea how long he had been asleep for, but when he awoke it was dark and late in the evening. Although the rain had subsided, he was still completely soaked.

The city looked alive and lit up, the light from its neon signs reflected in the recently formed puddles.

Dallas eased his way up to his feet. His body still ached, stiff and sore, and further exacerbated by the wet and cold. It hurt to take his first steps, but he soon walked out of the pain and onto the seductive streets of the night.

Sallad and Frederick stood in Sallad's living room. It was exactly six in the evening, and the two talked about the previous session's occurrences.

"Sallad," Frederick said, "you can't continue doing bad things and inflicting violence on the guy. It will just harm the sequence. You're abusing it."

"Listen to yourself, Fred. You sound ignorant and uninformed. This Easton guy will not be damaged, because I have the control, not him. This is just the kind of test the Awakening needs. And do you really care what happens to some inconsequential planet like Earth?"

He did not give Frederick any time to respond.

"Once I'm done working out the kinks with this guy, we're going to the Awards. We'll be so powerful with this thing. We will have it all. Access to anything we could ever want or need. Now hook me in."

Frederick Norsle certainly did not agree with the idea of destroying Dallas's life through violence, but Sallad had made the glorious side of the sequence seem so glamorous that it was nearly impossible for him to resist.

He hooked Sallad up, and within minutes he had fallen asleep, and transplanted himself back into Dallas's world, ready to further inflict severe harm and destruction.

Dallas continued to exploit the network of side streets and alleyways to make his way through the city. As he maneuvered the back streets, he constantly kept his head down, chin tucked into his chest, in the hope of concealing himself as best as possible.

A car came to a sudden halt a few feet from Dallas.

"Get in. Quick," a voice stammered.

Startled, Dallas peered into the car and stood frozen upon recognizing the driver.

It was Brian.

"Brian," Dallas began, but he was interrupted.

"Don't talk. Just get in."

The two drove on for several blocks before either of them uttered a word. The quiet was due in part to the fact that Sallad was confused. He had thought Brian to be out of the picture, but he allowed the two to continue at their own pace.

Finally, Brian broke the silence, "Dallas, I don't know what's going on with you, but you're pretty screwed up. A lot of people are dead, and a lot are after you. You really messed up Stephen, and a lot of other good people."

Dallas cut him off, "Brian, please, you have to listen carefully to what I'm saying. You *must* believe me. That person who killed all those innocent people wasn't me. I mean, it was me in flesh, but something is controlling me. I have no idea when it happened, why, or what it is, but something is wrong."

"Then we will get you help."

"Brian, we can't go to the cops. Not right now, at least. I owe it to myself and those I've hurt to figure out exactly what's wrong with me. Once I do, I promise, then I will go to the authorities."

Brian looked at his friend with doubtful eyes.

Dallas continued, "All I know is that things started getting hazy the day you got fired and shot me."

"Dallas, stop! I already told you I don't know what you're talking about. Why would I shoot you? It's me, your best friend," Brian interjected.

"And fired? I mean, if my boss knew I was with you, I'd surely be fired. That's why it's crucial you turn yourself in. I promise we will get you whatever help you need, but you need to go to the police."

"I'm sorry, Brian. I can't do that. I just don't think you really understand what's happening. I don't know anything anymore," a sullen Dallas weakly replied.

Brian, a bit hesitant, reached over and placed an arm around Dallas, not sure if he would erupt or not.

Dallas continued, "I just woke up one day and went to work. The next thing I know, I'm some kind of awful and out-of-control maniac. Brian, I killed people! There's no coming back from that. Where can I even go? I got nowhere. Everyone wants me dead."

His best friend of years had no answers.

"I don't know," Brian simply said.

Sallad had had just about enough of this melodrama. He grew more concerned that Dallas might hint about some unknown force inside him, but at the same time did not feel threatened.

No one would ever believe a story like Easton's.

Sallad took control of the reins yet again and expeditiously transformed Dallas back into his puppet of destruction.

Dallas sprung across the seat and attacked Brian.

"Dallas! What are you doing!"

Dallas had both his hands firmly wrapped around Brian's throat. Brian tried his best to fight him off. The car swerved across three lanes, hopped the curb, and plowed onto the sidewalk before slamming into a couple on their evening stroll.

The vehicle's impact immediately killed the man and pinned the woman under its front-end. She cried out from the pain that erupted in her body.

Dallas continued to wail on Brian, each wallop inflicting more damage than the previous. Brian tried to tense up to absorb the blows, but he was too weak and had no response to counter Dallas's onslaught.

Dallas leaned into Brian and bit into his cheek. Brian couldn't even scream for help since his throat was choked. Dallas ferociously ripped his teeth from Brian's face and spat the torn flesh across the seat. Somehow possessing an innate familiarity with the vehicle, Dallas reached into the glove compartment and retrieved a heavy-duty flashlight packed with four D batteries.

Dallas raised the Maglite above his head. His hand slipped off Brian's throat.

"Dallas, please don't!"

Brian tried to shield his face, but his eyes filled with fear as the last thing he watched was the heavy weapon smash into his forehead, crushing his skull.

Dallas heaved a heavy sigh and laughed. Another one bites the dust.

Brian was dead.

Dallas casually got out of the car and sauntered over to the lady, who was still pinned against the shop's facade. She was on death's doorstep, and her screams had subsided as she had watched Dallas beat his best friend to death. Her labored breath slowed with each subsequent exhale she forced from her lungs.

The hour was late, and traffic was sparse. Dallas didn't think anyone had seen him, but who cared if they had.

He clubbed the old lady to death and left.

"Old hag," he laughed as he walked away.

Dallas continued towards a row of buildings down the street. He had no idea where he was headed. His gait was slow and erratic, almost like a zombie, and his eyes were cold and empty. He was completely powerless to the effects of the sequence.

A police car careened around the corner as the blare of its sirens pierced through the otherwise calm night. Moments later, several more squad cars also raced around the corner.

Easton started running.

"This is the police, stop running and lay down. You're surrounded," a cop boomed over his speaker.

Dallas ignored the voice and kept running. He skipped through an alley and came across a grassy plot of land sandwiched between two buildings. There were two more cruisers waiting for him on the other side.

He ran as fast as he could to an apartment building that was no more than fifteen yards away. He jumped to the fire escape and quickly scampered up to the roof.

A dozen police officers were now circling the area below him. They all had their guns drawn, desperately hoping to get Easton in their scopes. A few of them hopped up on the escape and started to give chase while several more stormed through the front door. The rest secured the area.

Once Dallas reached the roof, he kicked out a window and crashed through the shattered pane and into the attached apartment. A woman screamed and ran from the room into her bedroom. Dallas chased after her.

She reached into a dresser drawer and pulled out a handgun. As she turned around to shoot Dallas, he leapt at her and swiped the gun. He stood over her and fired a single shot from point-blank range. He then grabbed a box of ammo, also in the drawer, and stuffed a handful of bullets into his pockets. He stormed out of the room and into the adjoining hall.

A message crackled across all the walkie-talkies, "This is the chief. Proceed with caution, shots have been fired. Shoot to kill. I repeat, shoot to kill."

One cop yelled to his partner, "Let's bury this bastard. He's a damn animal!"

The stairwell door at the end of the hall flew open. Several cops, armed to the teeth, carefully stepped into the hallway.

Dallas was able to duck between a bank of vending machines before they laid eyes on him.

The apartment building was quite large in stature,

and Sallad was supremely confident he could maneuver Dallas to evade law enforcement.

As the officers continued down the hall, they swept their guns side to side, ready to take out anything that crossed their path.

Once they were a few feet from his hiding spot, Dallas jumped out and fired before they even knew what had happened. He got off two shots with the precision of a marksman, striking each cop square in the throat.

He scurried back into the room he had originally entered and exited through the window onto the roof. His body began to tremble uncontrollably.

"Sallad, wake up," Frederick said frantically as he shook Sallad. "I have to tell you something important about the sequence."

A stunned Sallad was jolted from his slumber.

"Fred, what the hell are you doing?"

"Sallad, you can't be using the sequence as much as you are! You will burn it out. You're exerting too much kinetic power into the transfer. There's too much electricity for the computer to comprehend! You have to cool it for a few days."

"Fred, I'm in the middle of a sequence right now. I need to continue. I can't just stop."

"Yes, you can. Just shut it off and let fate take its natural course. Otherwise, things will become much too unstable if you don't."

"No! This is my sequence! I discovered it, and I'll

be damned if I let someone else tell me when I can and can't run it!" Sallad was furious.

Defiant, he placed the headring back on.

Suddenly, Norsle erupted, grabbed Sallad by the collar, and jerked him out of the chair.

"Listen, you ignorant prick, it was me who helped you finalize this thing. It was me you told to govern the logistics. And now it's me telling you to stop!"

Sallad was shocked by Frederick's sudden and explosive change in demeanor.

"I know that the only thing you're using this for is to create havoc. I admit I too was caught up with it, but we're done for now. It's far too dangerous."

Sallad charged his friend and knocked him to the ground. He rammed a knee into Norsle's stomach.

"You wanted this just as bad! You volunteered to assist, so don't start giving me orders, telling me to shut it off!"

"Sallad, look at you," Frederick pleaded, "you're letting it run your life. Now stop, or I have no choice but to report you to Ethic Crimes."

"You wouldn't dare do that!"

"Just you watch me!" Frederick shouted back.

"They won't find it. I'll hide it and deny it."

Frederick landed a punch to Sallad's midsection and was able to wriggle out from beneath him. The two wrestled and exchanged wild punches while they rolled across the floor.

Frederick got to his feet and made a dash for the headring. Sallad unleashed a violent kick flush against Norsle's shin that hobbled him and sent him crashing back to the floor.

"You're not going anywhere," Sallad said, getting to his feet.

Frederick grabbed at his lower leg and moaned.

"Sallad, please, stop! You're insane! Think about what you're doing."

Sallad kicked him in the ribs and went to kick him again, but before he could, Frederick grabbed his foot and yanked Sallad to the floor next to him. Norsle reached once more for the headring, and this time was successful in his attempt to seize it.

Unfortunately, he was unable to snap it, the wire material would not break. He scrambled to the computer and yanked out the connected wires.

Frederick didn't see Sallad rise to his feet.

Neither did he see him grab his "Employee of the Year" marble statuette off the shelf.

But the last thing Frederick did see was complete darkness as Sallad slammed the heavy chunk of rock into the back of Frederick's head, instantly ending his life.

Dallas crashed to the ground as the pursuing cop grabbed him and tackled him to the pavement. Once on the ground, the cop pistol-whipped the back of Dallas's head and knocked him out.

CHAPTER 15

Once again, Dallas found himself asleep on a cold and uncomfortable floor. This time it was that of the prisoner transport truck, on its way to Ironwood Penitentiary.

The ride was extremely bumpy and very rough. There were no main highways that led directly to the prison and so the armed vehicle was forced to maneuver third-rate roads that were uneven and long overdue for maintenance. Nonetheless, Dallas was out cold, due to the heavy amount of tranquilizer he had been given.

Sallad stared down at Frederick's lifeless body.

The moment had happened so quickly, and Sallad still found himself shocked and dazed from what had just transpired.

He had just killed Frederick Norsle.

His best friend, and companion in completing the Awakening's final initiation process, lay dead on his floor.

And why?

Because he didn't want Sallad to abuse the sequence and overpower it with his warped intentions.

Sallad had no idea what to do with the corpse. His mental state was clouded. He was so mixed up and turned around, that the only thing he thought to do was plug all the disconnected wires back into the computers.

He placed the headring on his head and resumed the sequence.

Dallas blinked his eyes open.

The first thing he noticed was two sets of ankles resting on the floor in front of him.

He tried to move.

"Hey, looks like our psycho friend is awake," one of the guards said, nudging the other with his elbow.

The other guard snorted, "We'll just have to do something about that now, won't we."

The guard smashed the butt of his rifle right between Dallas's stoned eyes. His head bounced off the truck's filthy floor. His vision immediately went screwy.

Before he could recover, a steel-tipped toe crashed into the side of his stomach, knocking the wind out of him. Dallas crunched his body together and violently coughed in pain. One of them landed a heel on the back of Easton's neck, causing his body to flatten across the floor.

The guards were unrelenting.

The sliding panel separating the front seat and the prisoner cabin slid open.

"What's going on back there?" a voice asked.

"Our friend here decided it was time to wake up, we're just helping him back to bed."

"Yeah, well keep him alive until Ironwood, then you can do as you please."

The panel slid shut. Each guard kicked Dallas in the abs one final time for good measure before sitting back down on the metal bench.

Dallas Easton, a confused and helpless man, at the mercy of another's control, lay half dead on the floor of a prison transport vehicle, a few miles from the toughest penitentiary in the country, for unspeakable crimes that he committed, but that his mind could not comprehend or rationalize.

Is there no longer a God?

There was in Dallas's world.

His name was Sallad.

Sallad continued to frantically push buttons and flip switches on the various machines, but to his dismay, nothing happened. Frustrated, he checked and rechecked the power box to ensure everything was still plugged in.

After examining the plethora of power cords and cables that streamed from the box, he concluded his final and only option was to reboot the sequence.

He kneeled in front of his computer, which had

tumbled to the floor during the fray, and typed away on the keyboard. He shut down the entire system, waited a minute, and booted everything back up.

He then entered the numerical code, 412219, to access the Awakening sequence.

Due to his cloudy and compromised state of mind, which was still trying to process what happened with Frederick, Sallad did not realize the fatal error he had just committed.

He had accessed the sequence with the code that could only be used to create instructions, and never to access the file.

Unbeknownst to him, he had just destroyed his ability to control the sequence.

He put the headring back on and took a seat in the comforchair.

The prison truck slowly turned onto a rough and narrow gravel driveway and continued for several miles before it arrived at the facility checkpoint.

Heavily armed guards loomed everywhere. Men were situated on the lookout towers, rooftops, driveway, and along the fenced perimeter.

This was Ironwood, the nation's toughest penal institution.

In its entire existence, there had never been an escape from the place. There had been three attempts, all three prisoners shot down, dead.

No one messed with Ironwood.

The transport vehicle's metal doors clanged open.

"On your feet, Easton. Now. This ain't no playground, boy, this is Ironwood. Welcome home!"

A reception of armed guards greeted Dallas as he was pushed out of the truck. The horde surrounded him and began to taunt him.

"So you're the big, tough, scary man."

"How's it feel to be a rat in a cage?"

"You're on our time now, pretty boy."

One of the guards planted his billy club into Dallas's rib cage. Still dazed, Easton fell to the ground coughing. As he coughed, with each breath he inhaled a mouthful of dirt that swirled across the hot ground.

He felt like he could puke at any moment.

The waning effects of the sedative that had been administered left him unsteady as he tried to get to his feet, and he again collapsed to the gravel.

"Pick the bum up and take him to Block C, we about to initiate this boy," one of the men said.

The posse of security guards accompanied Dallas to the entrance of Ironwood. A loud buzzer sounded, and they then proceeded through the towering iron gates and into a courtyard. They cleared a second set of iron gates before entering the stone fortress.

Once inside, Easton was escorted into a room with four glass walls where he was ordered to strip naked.

As soon as the door slammed shut, torrents of ice-cold water pelted him from the overhead sprinklers.

Dallas immediately began to hyperventilate.

The frigid shower continued for a minute before abruptly changing to a warmer temperature. The sudden transition in temperature confused his mind, making it believe his body was being scalded with hot water.

He screamed out in pain as the onlooking guards laughed and mocked him.

After the sprinklers had subsided, a door opposite the one he entered swung open. Another herd of armed guards waved Dallas through and tossed him a towel. They threw him a pair of grays, Ironwood's standard uniform, and told him to get dressed.

"Welcome to Ironwood," a guard snickered.

CHAPTER 16

Dallas Easton was now an inmate at Ironwood, and in all likelihood, the penitentiary would be his home for the rest of his life.

He would never see civilization again.

Upon his arrival and after his "shower," Dallas was led down a dimly lit corridor and shoved into an empty room. The room was completely white and had a very obscure shape to it. Easton didn't know what to make of the odd layout, but he was sure there was some sinister reason for its architecture.

Sallad tried to readjust the headring.

He still had no idea that moments earlier he had inadvertently destroyed the sequence when he used the wrong passcode to access it.

Again, he firmly secured the headring and flipped

on the Interface.

Immediately, the machine shorted itself, creating an electrical disturbance that affected all the equipment in the room. An extremely painful tremor ripped its way through Sallad's skull. The room plunged into darkness as every piece of hardware powered down. He tore the headring from his stinging head and whipped it across the room, smashing it against the wall.

As Dallas paced the obscurely designed room, he was suddenly overpowered by a surge of electricity that coursed throughout his entire body. It stunned him, and instantly dropped him to the floor.

Sallad struggled to figure out what went wrong. Still reeling from the effect of the shock, he powered the computer back on, hoping, just maybe, it was only a glitch.

Dallas's mind spun violently like a centrifuge as he lay on the floor staring up at the pristine white ceiling of the cellblock. Although he was on his back, a severe bout of dizziness had him thinking he was going to fall over as he watched the room whiz by. He tried to close his eyes, but it only made things worse.

Sallad stumbled over to the fax machine and wrenched the intra-circuit wire from it. Perhaps if he tried connecting the other end to the headring it would work.

Dallas squeezed his eyes closed as tightly as he could in hopes of alleviating the dizziness. An image of a giant halo of white dots forming a weblike structure invaded his mind.

Sallad collapsed to the floor due to the intense whirling sensation he felt inside his head.

Dallas tried to open his eyes but couldn't. Flashes of Tom, Stephen, Brian, and the multitude of other lives he had wreaked havoc upon streamed across his field of vision.

Unbeknownst to either of them, the energy fields of two opposing galaxies, billions of miles apart, had just been crossed, tearing a hole in the space-time continuum fabric of the universe.

Suddenly, Dallas experienced a vision of a person he knew to be the force that had been controlling him.

It was an exact replica of himself!

He opened his eyes.

Dallas Easton was lying in a field on the planet of Epacseon, the result of an energy overload that disrupted the equilibrium component of the Awakening.

* * *

A benefit of the celestial transportation Dallas had just experienced, was that he had been granted some type of omniscient intelligence. The sequence had reversed itself and everything suddenly made complete sense.

It was Dallas who now had control over Sallad. And each time he closed his eyes an even clearer image of his nemesis appeared.

Unfortunately, Dallas was also fully aware that

because the sequence had been inverted, it meant he could never venture back to Earth.

His new home was Epacseon.

No longer dizzy or disoriented, Easton felt more energized and invigorated than he had at any other point in his life that he could remember.

He hopped to his feet.

Dallas was in no hurry as he meandered along the superhighway towards the magnificent and shiny, silver outline of the city.

The task at hand was as clear to him as the Epacseon sky; find his parallel self, the evil inverse who was Sallad.

Somewhere inside that utopia, Sallad surveyed the mess that existed within his living room walls. All his machines were fried and no longer functioned. And the only person who could possibly help him lay dead on the floor amid the clutter.

Sallad was spent.

His brain felt scrambled. He needed to escape the present scene and get somewhere where he could collect his thoughts. He grabbed his briefcase, stuffed all his papers in it, and left for his office.

Dallas was unsure how long he had been walking, but it felt like time had quickly passed. Perhaps because he was enamored with the city that stretched out before him, and in awe of his surroundings. He had never seen anything like this before.

Epacseon resembled something straight out of a dream, something Earthlings simply couldn't create.

It was the quintessential Green World.

A hover transport cruised overhead. Dallas smiled at its sleekness and sophistication. The planet's technology was mind-boggling and well beyond the comprehension of most people.

Everything he saw amazed him.

It was very sunny and bright and green. There was an abundance of lush foliage in almost every direction. The sky was the perfect shade of cobalt to showcase the Tullib with its red glow and ever-present warmth.

He liked it here.

And at that moment, both he and Sallad were on their way into the heart of the city.

CHAPTER 17

I t didn't take long for Sallad to arrive at his office. The ride into the city did little to ease his mind and he still found himself in an exhausted and confused state.

He had barely slept in a few days. Every time he closed his eyes, he was awake living someone else's life.

The hover door opened and Sallad stepped onto his floor. It was an Offday and only a handful of individuals were at the office, one of whom was Herbert Ritke, the gentleman who had been promoted over Sallad, since Sallad had been MIA the previous week for no reason.

Sallad entered his office.

Dallas was awestruck as he entered the city limits.

The tall buildings dwarfed any skyline he had ever seen on Earth.

Although there were automobiles on Epacseon, everywhere he looked he watched transports zoom across the sky at altitudes as low as thirty feet.

Dallas closed his eyes. He envisioned Sallad in his office, sitting behind his desk. He conjured up an image of Sallad lying on the ground.

The canteen was closed and Sallad needed an energy boost. He reached down beside him to open a file cabinet where he kept his Gotcha. As he reached for the canister, he slipped from his chair and tumbled to the floor. He landed with a loud thud that drew a glance from the temp at the reception desk. She poked her head up over the counter and peeked through the glass walls into Sallad's office. She passed off one of those polite smiles, the kind that all secretaries are taught. Sallad offered a halfhearted smile in return.

Dallas took his time as he ambled through the downtown area of the city, which was intertwined with the largest park he had ever seen. There had to be at least a thousand acres of trees and undulations. He had never seen anything like it. Then again, he had never seen anything like Epacseon.

In one section of the park was a humongous decorative waterspout built atop a mound. Every few minutes the fountain would propel columns of water fifty stories high for a minute at a time, during which time little kids would stand under the spray and shriek in delight.

Amazingly, the water landed directly back into the

nozzles from which it had spewed, as if to misplace not even a single drop. Recycling was big on Epacseon, and nothing was ever wasted, not even water.

Dallas continued into the heart of the city before he decided to stop into a small shop resembling a deli. He took a seat at the counter and ordered a cup of Gotcha.

"Excuse me, what time is it?" he asked the server.

"Thirty-one," the guy responded.

Dallas had no idea what that meant but figured it best to not ask and just try to blend in. The clothes Dallas wore were similar to how others were dressed, except for the fact that on Offdays, no one wore buttons.

Dallas took a sip of the brew that sat on the counter. He immediately coughed and spit the stuff back into his cup. Gotcha was a powerful substance, not for first-timers.

"You okay, buddy?" the server asked. "You seem a bit edgy. How about some fricticity?"

"Sure," Dallas said, having no idea what he'd just said yes to.

The server placed something that could only be described as some type of a thick and concentrated juice concoction in front of Dallas.

"Thanks," Dallas said with a smile.

As he looked around the room, he couldn't help but notice that everyone was extremely chipper and had a smile on their face.

So far, Dallas liked it on Epacseon. Although he

had just arrived on the planet, he seemed to have assimilated quite a bit already. He found the climate to be very comfortable as it never changed, not even when the Tullib recharged itself.

Dallas finished the juice and left.

Sallad laid his head down on his desk. In less than a minute, he was asleep. A vision flashed across his eyes of a man walking out from a canteen.

It was Dallas.

Immediately, Sallad jerked his head up from the desk.

"Dallas!" he exclaimed.

Impossible, he wasn't even hooked up. He closed his eyes again and saw him.

"I must need more sleep," he murmured, "I can't be seeing him. He seems so real and so near."

Sallad was not hallucinating.

The newly arrived visitor from Earth was less than two blocks away from Sallad's building and getting closer with every step he took.

And Easton knew exactly where he was headed.

CHAPTER 18

Dallas stood on the grassy concourse at the base of the gargantuan glass building where Sallad worked. He marveled at its sheer size and the way its mirrorlike finish reflected the Tullib's light.

Sallad frantically paced the floor of his office, fully aware Dallas was coming for him. Somehow, he needed a discrete exit from the building, and then he had to disappear for a while.

He grabbed a folder and left.

Dallas entered the lobby through one of the building's many sets of glass doors. The large, open atrium was beautiful, reminding him somewhat of the multi-storied shopping malls he would see on Earth.

The building towered upwards as far as his eye could see. Tall trees also stretched up along its interior and each floor was surrounded by an exterior walkway.

As Dallas looked around, he swore that during regular Ondays the office building could accommodate at least a million people.

A twisted sense of exuberance filled Dallas.

He knew where Sallad was.

Finally, he was close to confronting the man who destroyed his life.

Sallad jumped into the hoverport and rode it to the lobby. The doors opened and he suddenly found himself staring directly at Dallas.

The pair locked eyes.

Although they had only seen each other in their dreams, they might as well have been staring into a mirror.

They were identical in every physical facet.

Sallad anxiously stabbed at the button to close the door, desperately jamming it with his finger until it finally started to close.

Dallas sandwiched a hand between the elevator's closing doors. He made quite a commotion as he tried to force open the heavy doors, causing those around to glance over at what was happening.

Sallad repeatedly punched Dallas's arm until it recoiled and the doors closed. Sallad didn't know what button he had pushed, but the hover shot up.

Dallas jumped in the adjoining hover and pushed a button. The hovers were constructed of glass, and the men glared at each other as they zoomed past floor after floor and continued to rise higher.

Suddenly, Dallas's lift came to an abrupt halt at one of the floors. He watched as Sallad continued to shoot upwards at a rapid rate.

Damn.

The door opened and two girls tried to step into the hover, but Dallas prevented them from boarding and pressed a button to a much higher level. Sallad's hover halted at floor 877. Dallas watched Sallad exit. He realized he would need to backtrack, costing him valuable time.

Sallad ran through the halls as he tried to come up with a plan. He ducked into a utility closet, shut the door, and maneuvered his way around some of the cleaning supplies. He slid down against the wall and huddled in the corner. He wrapped his arms around his knees as he closed his eyes.

After what seemed like an eternity, Dallas finally stormed out of the elevator onto floor 877.

Sallad remained quiet as he sat still in the dark of the room, alone with only the blackness to keep him company.

Dallas turned the corner and slowed his run to a walk. He didn't need to draw more attention to himself.

His head was on a swivel as he looked for Sallad.

Easton stopped and stood in the middle of the hall at an intersection. People had to step out of the way as he just stood there and patiently waited. Finally, he stepped on the hover and proceeded to the next floor.

Sallad had fallen asleep and lost track of how long he had been in the closet. He carefully opened the door and peeked his head out into the empty hallway.

There was no one on the floor.

He crept from the storage closet and moved towards the slideway. It would take him much longer to get down to the main level using the electric slideway, but he needed to stay clear of the visibility the hover afforded.

After descending thirty flights, Sallad grew impatient and opted to risk the rest of the descent using the hover. He had to move fast. His uneasy feeling that Dallas could be anywhere in the building intensified.

A week earlier, Sallad had been a respected technoscientist, a Harnesser worthy of the esteem most of his colleagues bestowed on him. However, he had let himself morph into a villainous and diabolical individual.

That same evil individual now cowered like a baby as he waited for the hover. He felt like a hunted rat.

The door opened and Sallad quickly stepped into the hover transport. He pressed the button for Floor 47, which was ground-level, and was immediately whisked down to the lobby.

The hover moved exceptionally fast since there were no other individuals to interrupt its progress.

Sallad stepped out of the machine. Just as the door was closing, he thrust his forearm back into the hover to prevent its full closure.

He had forgotten his briefcase.

All his papers and research on the Awakening sequence were in there, and he could not take the risk of someone accidentally stumbling upon them.

He had no choice. He had to go back.

Sallad made it back up to his floor in a record time of fifty-six seconds. The mile-and-a-half rapid ascent left him slightly lightheaded. He staggered to his office. The entire floor was dark, save for the light cast off by the slideway exit signs.

He pressed his face against the glass wall of his office and was able to make out the silhouette of his briefcase on the chair.

After fumbling around in his pockets for his identity card, he ran it through the scanner and the door unlocked. Sallad made a beeline straight to the briefcase. He grabbed it, turned around, and immediately gasped.

Dallas Easton was standing in the doorway.

CHAPTER 19

"Hello, Sallad. I can't express how nice it is to finally meet you. It's funny though, because in some ways it feels like I've known you all my life," Dallas laughed sardonically.

"Who are you? What do you want from me?" a frightened Sallad asked, trying to play dumb.

"Why, I'm you. And you were me, at least for a little while anyway. You of all people should know who I am. Aren't you going to welcome me in?" Easton retorted.

"Listen, I don't know what you want, but if you don't leave immediately, I'll call security."

"Go ahead, Sallad, but you know how mean I can get. Or maybe that's you who gets mean. I still haven't quite figured that part out yet."

Dallas entered the office and locked the door.

Dallas continued, "See, I've been trying to figure this whole thing out and I'm having a little trouble trying to decipher all this. As you know, Sallad, I come from Earth, and we are not nearly as advanced as you Epacseonites."

Easton flipped on the Interface's monitor, "Let's take a little gander, shall we?"

"I have no idea what you're looking for or hoping to find," Sallad replied.

Dallas got up and grabbed Sallad by the neck. Sallad was no wimp though, and he grabbed Dallas's hand and wrenched it free from his neck.

"Leave me alone," Sallad stammered.

"Sit down and show me what you've done to me," Easton fired back as he pointed at the machine. "Surely, you with all your awards and prestige must have one hell of a program on that thing. Open it up now!"

"Screw you! You ignorant troglodyte," Sallad snapped back.

Dallas pounded his fist onto the desk so hard that the machine bounced up half an inch and most of the desk supplies fell onto the floor. He grabbed a paperweight off the desk and heaved it at the window. It smashed into the glass leaving only a small scratch on the thick pane.

"Did I not make myself clear!" he screamed.

Sallad could see the rage in Dallas's eyes and knew he had to tread carefully. He did not know exactly how much power the Awakening had transferred.

He activated the program on his Interface.

Dallas loomed over him, watching as the screen populated with various information. Finally, one word appeared in the center of the monitor: AWAKENING.

"Show me what you did to me."

Sallad had no choice. He knew that Easton could kill him at any moment due to the fact he still had various instructions imprinted inside his mind. They were still capable of activating even though the machine had been destroyed.

He laughed to himself and figured he had nothing to lose. He was going to be fired and disgraced among the Harnessing community. He had no way to prove that the sequence had worked. And at some point, it would be discovered that he had murdered Frederick Norsle.

Why not tell Dallas everything?

"To begin," Sallad said, "it was my intention to design a program in which the administrator could control the dreams of an individual."

"You mean mess with their minds," Dallas quickly interjected.

"No. That wasn't the intention. I thought it would be fascinating to be able to help someone enter a deep state of somnia through specifically tailored dreams. Only, there were other factors that had to be tested beforehand. I had no idea what the consequences could be, and I'm still not even sure how you were brought into the picture."

"You're lying!"

"I swear to you that's the truth," Sallad lied.

Dallas grew more agitated. It wasn't hard to see right through Sallad's deceitfulness.

"You ruined me! You made me a monster! I was a good person! You took all that from me!"

"Fine! You want to know? You really want to know?" Sallad yelled back.

At this point Sallad knew Dallas would probably try to kill him anyway. Why not go down swinging?

"You're right, I ruined you! I destroyed your life. I created a series of sequences that would allow me to hijack the mind of anyone I chose and impose my will upon them." He was relishing the chance to finally share his secret with someone.

Sallad continued his rant, "And I chose you as my pathetic little puppet! With a little help from a colleague, I was able to jump into your consciousness and take control of your insignificant life! I became you!"

The rage harboring within Dallas boiled over. He charged Sallad and exploded into him, knocking him to the ground.

Sallad didn't even have time to try to avoid him.

Dallas grabbed him by the collar and shook him violently, banging his head over and over against the hard floor.

"You son of a bitch, you ruined my life!" Dallas screamed. "You had no right! You had no right!"

Dallas bellowed at the top of his lungs.

The dam had broken.

His pent-up aggression could no longer be contained by any office space. His screams blasted through the walls, echoed across the floor, and spilled into the openness, finally being muffled by the trees that sprouted in the center of the building.

Dallas let go and watched Sallad fall limp.

Sallad, barely conscious, laughed maniacally, "I really messed you up man. You're done. You can't ever go back."

Dallas's rage reignited itself. He grabbed Sallad once more.

"Yes, I can."

"No, you can't," Sallad chortled in a shrill tone.

"You're gonna help me, then I'm gonna kill you."

"Hahaha! You can't go back. I don't know what happened to get you here, but you're stuck. I destroyed the machine, you're stuck!"

"I'll make your partner help me"

"Oh sure, good luck with that. I killed him. Or was it you?" Sallad chuckled even louder.

A visage of resignation overtook Dallas.

Sallad kept at the badgering, "It doesn't matter, you're trapped! Welcome to Epacseon!"

"Epacseon," Dallas repeated.

"No escape." Sallad grinned.

Dallas got up off the floor, ran his hands through his hair, and gripped tight around the back of his head.

He was trapped.

And he knew it.

There was absolutely no way he could leave.

Sallad also managed to get to his feet. He stared into the face of his twin.

"Hey," he laughed, "look at the bright side, you get to be another me haha..."

Dallas rushed Sallad and threw him up against the window. An overload of adrenaline flowed through him. It made him mean. Meaner than Sallad had ever made him. These were now his own feelings and emotions.

"I'm gonna kill you," he screamed and punched Sallad in the nose.

Sallad shielded his face with his hands.

Dallas kneed him squarely in the groin and, as Sallad doubled over, delivered a fierce blow with his elbow sending the deviant to the floor.

He jumped on Sallad and threw every punch and kick he had at him. Dallas grabbed the paperweight off the floor and began beating Sallad with it.

Any hope Dallas ever had of retaining his decency was gone.

Sallad shrieked in agony as he absorbed the ferocious assault. He too was a goner, and his laughs turned into mumble jumble as the damage to his brain intensified.

Dallas grabbed the Interface and wrenched it off the desk, and in doing so yanked its cords from the wall's outlet, which caused a small spark.

He then slammed the machine down onto Sallad.

The spark ignited a small flame inside the wall that quickly engulfed the expansive circuitry wired within its confines. Seconds later, the entire inner core of the office was ablaze. The fire spread like spilt gasoline and within seconds the entire perimeter of the room was a massive ring of fire.

There was no way to evade the inferno that soon encompassed the entire space.

But Dallas didn't care.

He continued to unleash the vehemence inside him on Sallad. As he beat him, Sallad's eyes rolled back into his head, fluttering back and forth.

"You. Want. To. Be. Me!" Easton screamed. "You want to know what I think, well here you go. Have a new mind. Or better yet, an open mind."

Dallas repeatedly smashed Sallad's head into the enormous window. The thick glass pane started to crack with each jarring blow, and the cracks quickly developed into a weblike maze and began to spread across the glass.

Dallas refused to let up.

The top of Sallad's head was a tangled mess of blood-soaked hair and excoriated skin.

CRACK!

The entire window wall came crashing down.

The glass cascaded onto Sallad and its weight swept his body right out the window with it, crashing toward the pavement hundreds of stories below.

Dallas watched his body's freefall until the tiny outline of Sallad's figure disappeared from his view.

The fire was almost on top of Dallas.

There was only one thing left to do.

Dallas Easton stepped onto the window ledge and leapt out. And in doing so, he followed Sallad's path from the heights of Epacseon, straight into the depths of misery.

CHAPTER 20

The loud and obnoxious shrill of the alarm clock pierced the morning stillness and filled the room with its unpleasant tone.

Dallas Easton, awakened by an intense feeling of freefall, glanced at the alarm clock. It was 7:38 on a Friday morning. Dallas reached over and shut off the alarm clock.

In the kitchen, Dallas flipped on the television to listen to the morning news program as he prepared his usual breakfast of two eggs and a mug of black coffee.

"Again, to recap our top story, astronomers have discovered a previously uncharted planet, billions of miles from Earth," the news anchor excitedly reported. "The scientific community is abuzz, as initial reports suggest that this planet might just be able to sustain life. In other news, it's going to be a hot one out there today..."

ACKNOWLEDGMENTS

I'd be remiss if I did not thank Joseph Toner, my high school English teacher, right off the bat. Without him, this story would most likely not exist. It was Mr. Toner who helped instill in me a love of creative writing, and the idea that the right words, in the right order, could have a profound and lasting effect.

To my family-thank you for your unwavering love and support. It's been quite a journey, one that none of us ever envisioned. We have survived some of life's tough tests and grown closer as a result. I know in my heart that I would not be where I am today if I did not have you in my life.

To Perry and Miller-you both get your own special acknowledgment. You will probably never come close to comprehending the level of joy you have brought to my life. Every moment I spend with you is a moment I treasure and thank the Lord for. I am proud to be your uncle and Godfather.

To all my friends-and you know who you are. Thank you for being there when I need you. I have relied on you for quite a bit, and it's my hope that I am able to return the favor.

To my nurses and caregivers-thank you for showing up. Not just physically, but for accompanying me throughout this journey and going above and beyond when needed. I don't know what shape I'd be in if not for your continued care. I consider you some of my best friends.

To the others who helped me with this book in one way or another-Brooks Becker for another thorough copyedit; Ryan Mulford for designing a kick ass cover that delivered the look I was going for; to those who offered me a bit of advance praise and an endorsement; to the folks at Coyote Crest for believing that the crazy idea of publishing a high school writing assignment could prove to be worth the risk.

Finally, to you, the reader. Thank you for spending your hard-earned cash on this whimsical idea of a story. I hope you enjoyed it. And if you didn't, I'm sorry, but no refunds.

ABOUT THE AUTHOR

Scott Wiley Fedor is an inspirational speaker, disability advocate, and author. His best-selling memoir, *Head Strong: How a Broken Neck Strengthened My Spirit* has inspired thousands across the globe. *The Awakening* is his first published work of fiction. He currently resides in Cleveland, Ohio.

scottwfedor.com
@scottwfedor

www.ingramcontent.com/pod-product-compliance
Lightning Source LLC
Chambersburg PA
CBHW030959210726
48290CB00007B/2377